D1006634

LANDING GEAR

KATE PULLINGER

A Touchstone Book

PUBLISHED BY SIMON & SCHUSTER

New York London Toronto Sydney New Delhi

Touchstone
A Division of Simon & Schuster, Inc.
1230 Avenue of the Americas
New York, NY 10020

Copyright © 2014 by Kate Pullinger
Originally published in 2014 by Doubleday Canada

First Touchstone hardcover edition May 2014

TOUCHSTONE and colophon are registered trademarks of Simon & Schuster, Inc.

For information about special discounts for bulk purchases, please contact Simon & Schuster Special Sales at 1-866-506-1949 or business@simonandschuster.com.

The Simon & Schuster Speakers Bureau can bring authors to your live event. For more information or to book an event contact the Simon & Schuster Speakers Bureau at 1-866-248-3049 or visit our website at www.simonspeakers.com.

Jacket design by Rex Bonomelli
Jacket photograph © Andreia Takeuchi/Flickr Select/Getty Images

Manufactured in the United States of America

10   9   8   7   6   5   4   3   2   1

Library of Congress Cataloging-in-Publication Data
Pullinger, Kate.
Landing gear : a novel / Kate Pullinger.
      pages   cm
1. Life change events—Fiction. 2. Family life –Fiction. I. Title.
PR9199.3.P775L36   2014
813'.54—dc23
2013043608

ISBN 978-1-4767-5137-5
ISBN 978-1-4767-5138-2 (ebook)

For my family: Simon, Tom, and Iris

And for all the strangers who greet one another with
tenderness and hospitality

AUTHOR'S NOTE

I first came across the stories of landing gear stowaways in an article in the *Guardian* newspaper in 2001. A body had landed in a supermarket car park in London, not far from where I live. The two investigative journalists working on the story discovered that this young man was only the latest in a series of airplane stowaways to fall into or near this car park over the previous decade, released as planes lowered their wheels before landing. The journalists traced the identity of this most recent stowaway, traveling to Pakistan to meet his family. A myth circulates in some parts of the world that you can climb into the hold of an airplane via the landing gear. In fact, most people who attempt to stow away in this manner die en route, crushed by the enormous wheels of the plane as the landing gear retracts, or freezing to death once the plane reaches cruising altitude. But occasionally, people survive these extraordinary journeys and manage to reach their longed-for destinations.

PROLOGUE

FLIGHT PATHS

SPRING 2012

I went to Dubai from my home in Pakistan because I heard I could earn good money.

There was a man in my village who had been working in the Emirates; he was injured on the building site where he worked when a section of scaffolding fell on his foot. He had a lot of stories about what life was like in the workers' camps, so I knew what to expect.

I liked the look of Dubai; I liked the idea of living in a place where everything was new. The plane was full of men like me, leaving home to work abroad, although I was one of the youngest. When we landed, we were transported to the camp where we were to live.

The conditions were not good—too many men. But I was happy, and when I got to the building site the next day—two hours by bus either way—I was happier still. I wanted to work. Now I had a job. Now I would be paid.

But it turned out that getting paid for the work I did was not as simple as I thought it would be.

At the airport, I followed the instructions Ameer had given me—for which I had paid the last of my Dubai money—and found the unlocked door that led outside to the planes. I had less than fifteen minutes after darkness fell to find the correct airplane.

I'd been home from Dubai for a while, but there was no work in Karachi. I told Raheela, my sister, I was going back to Dubai. We spent a long time over our good-byes. She could tell that something was up, but I told no one my real plans, not even her. We'd lost our parents when we were teenagers—our father in the 2005 Kashmir earthquake, our mother a year after that—so we were used to finding our own way. Even so, I found it hard not to cry when we parted.

From the ground, the planes looked enormous, their lights blinking in the dusk. The air stank of petrol and tires.

But I found the plane I wanted, and no one saw me. I climbed over the giant wheels and shimmied up the landing gear and folded myself onto the little shelf, which was exactly where Ameer had said it would be.

I have to go to the supermarket today, otherwise my family will starve.

Well, not starve, exactly. In the event of a war or cataclysm of some kind, there is enough food in the house to last for—how long? The pantry. The fridge. The storage jars. The cupboard full of breakfast cereal. The shelf of tins. The peas that have fallen out of their bag and are rolling around in the bottom drawer of the freezer. The tahini that is older than my teenaged child.

We would last at least one month, maybe even two, before we would have to eat those jars of red wine preserves given to me several years ago. Except that isn't the point. The fact that there is already a ton of food in my house and I am on my way to buy more is not the point.

While there are plenty of wars and cataclysms happening elsewhere, as far as I can see, stuck as I am in the one-way traffic system, Richmond is its usual placid, well-fed self this week.

The family expects meals. They know that fairies do not replenish the cupboards in the night, but how, why, when, and where the food comes from is not something that interests them. It is not something that interests me either. But I am a good wife. I am a good mother.

DARK MASS

There is almost no room for me on this shelf;
there is no secret entrance into the cargo hold.

I finish the shopping beneath the supermarket's harsh
lights and zombie-walk Muzak; the boy at the checkout
is unaccountably cheerful, and this makes me smile.

I am crushed into this too-small space;
I have been here for an eternity.

I push the loaded trolley across the car park, battling to
keep its wonky wheels on track as it veers toward a row of
shiny bumpers.

Freezing hot, then burning cold.

I pop open the boot of my car and then for some reason,
I have no idea why, I look up, into the clear blue sky.

Suddenly, I am released.

And I see him.

Landing Gear

I am free.

It takes me a long moment to figure out what I am looking at.

I am flying.

A dark mass, growing larger quickly.

I am falling through the sky.

He is falling from the sky.

The earth is coming up to meet me.

I let go of the trolley and am dimly aware that it is getting away from me but I can't move, I am stuck in the middle of the supermarket car park, watching, as he hurtles toward me.

Almost there now, my destination.

I have no idea how long it takes—a few seconds, an entire lifetime—but I stand there holding my breath as the suburbs go about their business around me until . . .

I've arrived, at last.

He crashes into the roof of my car.

He looked perfect lying there, the roof of my car like a crumpled velvet blanket. I stood like an idiot and waited for people to gather round, waited for sirens to ring out, alarms to sound.

But there was only silence. The sound of my breathing. The sound of me staring. The sound of me not knowing what to do.

And then he sat up and said, in perfect, lightly accented English, "Am I dead?"

I nodded and tried to think of the right way to respond. "I think so. You must be. Or I am."

He climbed down off my car. "Is that your trolley?" He sprinted over to retrieve it without waiting for my reply. "Please take me with you. I'm starving."

"Okay," I said. "I've got food." The car was wrecked. "We'll get a taxi."

PART ONE

ASH CLOUD IDYLL

APRIL 2010

Later, much later, after it was too late and Harriet had too much time to dwell on it, she realized that it was all the fault of the planes. Everything that happened, all of it, all of the . . . stuff was the fault of the planes. Or rather, the fault of the volcano. If Eyjafjallajökull hadn't erupted, billowing into the jet stream vast plumes of ash laden with shards of ice, shutting down airspace over the whole of Europe, none of this would have happened. Jack wouldn't have been suspended from school; Michael wouldn't have spent that week in Toronto; Harriet would never have contacted George Sigo; she'd still have her job and her son would still believe that people are fundamentally decent. In the middle of April, life was normal; by the end of the first week of May, life had changed.

It was the day after the volcano erupted that Harriet noticed the sky. Extraordinary.

The day before, she'd been too caught up with the chaos in the radio newsroom as the airports had closed, one by one, north to south, like roman blinds being pulled down over the entire country: Glasgow—Edinburgh—Manchester—Birmingham—Heathrow—Gatwick. In order to read the news properly, she'd had to learn how to pronounce Eyjafjallajökull, along with a host of other Icelandic names. News bulletins had been bumped up from once an hour, to twice, to every fifteen minutes. She'd stayed late and left in a car her boss, Steve, ordered, the underground having long since stopped for the night. Once home, she found her son, Jack, asleep on the sofa, clutching his gaming handset, surrounded by pizza crusts, sticky glasses, and other debris.

The next morning she got up early. She'd slept well and felt a kind of lightness in her bones; she was clear-headed and unusually calm. She had a quick shower and put on a summer dress for the first time that year and this feeling of lightness continued and, if anything, amplified. She walked to the corner shop for milk and newspapers, but she'd only gone a few meters when she had to stop. The world felt entirely different. Spring had arrived and pink cherry blossoms carpeted the street. The air was luminous, the sky was clear. The neighborhood felt peaceful, the houses benevolent with their big clean windows and sturdy front doors. She hugged her cardigan around herself and began walking once again.

A moment later she realized what was different: there were no planes. Richmond had emerged from beneath the flight path. The air was sparkling. The sky was silent, completely silent.

Emily buried her father the day after the planes stopped flying. He had died the week before, a massive stroke that killed him instantly. He was sixty-one and had been a widower for many years. After taking early retirement from teaching maths at secondary school, he had lived on his own in the semidetached house in Shepherd's Bush, where Emily had grown up.

All the neighbors came to Chiswick New Cemetery to see Ted off. Turned out he'd had it all planned and paid for, including the custom-made coffin in the shape of a perch; he'd been a weekend angler all his life. The giant silver fish, Ted's final joke, startled his friends instead of amusing them, and they pretended it was nothing out of the ordinary, which Emily knew would have infuriated him. In an effort to cheer up everyone, Cory Newton, who had taught with Ted for many years, said, "He shouldn't be gone, but he did enjoy his life." Emily smiled at him miserably. Her face ached from crying and smiling, smiling and crying. One of Ted's neighbors, Karen, was set to deliver the graveside humanist eulogy Ted had requested, including a reading of Auden's "Stop All the Clocks"— "Ted's favorite poem," Karen said. "Ted's only poem," Cory replied. But when she got to the line "Let aeroplanes circle moaning overhead," Karen paused and looked up into the clear blue sky. There were no aeroplanes.

Emily felt her heart rip open in that moment, as though there was nothing between her and the endless, empty sky, as though God had stopped the planes as well as the clocks so that Ted could make his way to Heaven without being buffeted or damaged. Except she didn't believe in God and neither had Ted. In fact, looking around at the graveside gathering, Emily realized that probably no one present believed in any kind of God, except perhaps Monica and Tariq Hussein, but even with them she wouldn't have been surprised to learn that faith had slipped away.

The extraordinary silence and beauty of the day overwhelmed the people gathered there and instead of celebrating and honoring their lost friend—Emily's father in his sleek silver-scaled box—with stories and jokes and songs as he would have wanted, they were mired in misery.

Jack had lived through what felt like millions of school holidays, with their distinct combination of freedom and boredom, like a weekend that never ends, a whole string of exciting Saturdays that turn into dismal Sundays. The Easter holiday was always very long—sixteen days this year, Jack had counted—and his family hadn't gone away. Sometimes they did go away, Jack and his parents, city breaks in posh hotels with swimming pools. Why did his parents think that all he needed was a swimming pool to compensate for being dragged around endless churches, museums, and art galleries? But this year Jack's dad was in New York on business and Harriet was busy at the radio station.

Jack had spent all day Thursday on his games console, but today, Friday, he had big plans. His social circle had expanded over the year, this year, year nine, the third year of secondary school, and it now included girls as well as boys, and they did things together out in the world, with their free bus passes and the whole of London for them to explore. But they didn't explore the city, of course not, that would be boring. Instead they met up on the high street and hung out, spending their tiny allowances at McDonald's and KFC. From time to time, they took the bus or rode their bikes across the river to Dukes Meadows.

The first time Jack took the bus over to Dukes with his friends, he was nervous. It was a couple of months ago—he had recently turned fourteen and hadn't had a birthday party, the idea of birthday parties suddenly weird and childish. One of the girls—Ruby, no use pretending it was anyone other than Ruby—had suggested going to Dukes when it became apparent that none of them had enough money to buy a Coke in a shop, let alone at McDonald's, they'd been priced off the fucking high street. Jack and his friends got on the bus and headed over the river. Jack had a tingling sensation in his feet, this was new for him, he had never got on a bus with a bunch of other kids and headed off to an unknown destination—unknown to him but clearly well known to several of his friends.

They got off the bus and walked down the lane and it was as though they'd arrived in the countryside: there were allotments with shaggy old men bent low and digging, waiting for winter to end; there were women muffled in jackets and scarves, walking their dogs, their pockets stuffed with plastic bags; and then out on the common itself, the wet grass that hadn't been mowed in a while, seagulls, a couple of magpies, even a few ducks planting their flat feet in the mud as they made their way to the river. Dukes was not overlooked by flats and houses; it was not hemmed in by roads and walls; it was not surveyed by cameras; it was not supervised. The sky was huge, as were the trees, still winter-bare. The wind was cold coming off the river, and Jack and his friends huddled together in the old bandstand like a pack of shivering puppies.

Jack's dad had grown up in Canada and sometimes at Dukes Jack would wonder if this was what the whole of his father's childhood was like—one vast open space with huge empty skies full of weather. Jack's parents thought they knew what his life was like, but they had no idea. Jack imagined that in Canada everything was brand-new and clean and shiny, and everyone grew up like Jack's father, surrounded by kids who'd lived their whole lives just down the street. And Harriet, well, like Jack's dad she had grown up in the distant past before the internet, so she knew nothing.

The school Jack went to was old and shabby with narrow corridors that teemed with rough kids speaking too many languages, and rubbish all over the pavement, and nasty toilets with cracked sinks and wet toilet paper on the floor, and a roof that leaked because one night a gang stole the lead off it. Jack's friends were great, he loved his friends, but they were not from down the street, they were from Poland and Montenegro and Serbia and even Eritrea—their parents making new lives away from wars and unemployment.

Jack knew that he was lucky and that he had nothing to escape from, with his nice house, his kind father, and his mother who had nothing to do apart from worry about him. He knew he was better off than most. But fuck it. Being better off was not what mattered at the end of the day.

What did matter? Jack didn't know. Or rather, he didn't know yet. Sometimes he felt he had everything figured out, but then he realized he was mistaken. He knew things, of course, you can't get to fourteen without having learned a bunch of stuff, but he felt he didn't know anything important.

Now that it was spring, Dukes was even more appealing as the grass greened up and the trees began to put on leaves. Today's plan was to meet at twelve and head over to Dukes for the afternoon. On the high street he found his friends hanging out in front of the bus stop. They'd already pooled their cash and sent Louise to the shop behind the mini-cab stand where, rumor had it, girls could buy beer if they stuck out their boobs and were wearing lipstick.

"Louise doesn't need to stick out her boobs," said Frank, "they stick out enough already," and he laughed at his joke.

"Shut up, Frank," said Ruby.

Jack said, "Yeah, shut up, Frank."

"Ooh," said Frank, "Ruby has an echo. Little Echo Boy."

Jack thought about hitting Frank. He felt himself go red and he turned away from the group, as though he'd noticed something interesting across the street. Ruby was already ignoring them both, talking to her friend Saira, and Frank asked Jack if he had bought *FIFA 2010* yet, which Jack knew was his way of apologizing. Louise came skittering up the road, she'd managed to buy two cans of beer, and they got onto the bus and clambered upstairs, leery and shouty and full of themselves. At these times Jack felt self-consciously teenaged, like being a teenager was the most obvious, scripted, clichéd way of being in the world. Frank pushed him and he kicked Frank, and the look of horror in the old ladies' eyes made him cringe on the inside, but he laughed loudly and glanced to see if Ruby was watching. She wasn't.

At Dukes, the bandstand was already occupied by a bunch of kids from another school, older and rougher-looking, so they stayed well clear and moved over to the common instead. They opened the cans of beer and shared them round. Jack still wasn't sure about the taste, but at least he'd managed to move on from the massive involuntary shudders that used to overtake him whenever one of his parents offered him a sip. He liked the way the alcohol made him feel, how after a few glugs the band that was wound tight around his guts loosened a little, and the fear he had of saying or doing something wrong in front of his friends began to ease.

Today Ruby was sitting next to him and he was conscious of her leg touching his, but he could see that her other leg was touching Frank's. After they'd been there for a while and drunk the beer and discussed how much they hated their teachers and what a total plonker Mr. Evans was, and how Miss Gerhart showed too much crepey cleavage—"Her skin, man," said Frank, his face screwed tight with distaste, "it's like cowhide."

"Eww," said everyone else. Jack pressed his back

against the log he was leaning on and looked up at the sky. That's when he realized.

"No planes," he said.

"What—" Frank started with what Jack could hear was sarcasm, but he held up his hand and his gesture actually worked. Frank stopped speaking.

"Listen," said Jack, and he pointed upward. "No planes."

And they all looked up and they all remained silent, and for a moment Jack thought that, together, they'd seen God, but of course it was only the monumental shock of noticing the blue silent sky. Sometimes at Dukes the planes seemed so low that Jack felt that if he jumped high enough or stood on Frank's shoulders, he could reach up and brush his fingers along a plane's silvery undercarriage. But today the sky was empty.

"Freaky," said Frank after a while, and a collective shudder passed through them.

"A volcano," said Ruby.

"What?" asked Frank.

"A volcano in Iceland."

"This is what it will be like when we run out of oil," said Jack.

"He's seen the future, man," said Frank, "and it's bleak."

Ruby stood up as though she'd suddenly remembered she needed to leave. Jack began to stand as well but she pushed him back down, saying, "Wait, I've got something to show you." She ran out onto the damp grass and did a cartwheel.

Frank shouted, "The midget performs for us!"

They laughed, Ruby as well. It was true she was tiny, she hadn't grown at all over the past two, nearly three years, since they started secondary school, whereas Jack was growing so rapidly his friends claimed they could see him sprouting. Frank said he was doing a photography project, taking a picture of Jack every day and then running them together to create one of those YouTube time-lapse videos so that everyone in the world could see what a freak Jack was.

Ruby stood on the grass in front of them and shouted "Oi!" They stopped talking and looked at her obediently.

The silent sky brought with it a sense of occasion. Ruby sat down cross-legged. She jammed her hand in the pocket of her jacket and pulled out a sandwich bag full of marijuana.

At least, that's what Jack guessed it was, given that he had never seen a bag of marijuana before in real life. He corrected himself: "draw," that was what you were supposed to call it. Draw. She held it over her head and waggled it back and forth. "A gift from my big brother. A taster. For free."

For once, no one knew what to say.

"His evil plan," she added, "is to get you all hooked so that you become his devoted customers forevermore."

Pause. Then Frank spoke up. "Does he offer some kind of loyalty scheme?"

Moments later, as Jack inhaled for the first time through a taut mix of fear, desire, and curiosity, he thought, Am I doing this because there are no planes? Or would I be doing this anyway?

5

Work was frantic, everyone bursting with this weird news story, watching the satellite images as the ash cloud morphed, getting bigger and bigger, stretching south and east, covering more and more of Europe. Several reporters and presenters were away because of the school holiday, and with most European airspace shut, anyone abroad would now have difficulty returning home. With a jolt, Harriet realized that this presented her with an opportunity, a way to act on her desire, long dormant but still present: to get back into reporting after her years and years of continuity announcements, program links, and news reading. In her current job she did a bit of everything—writing the news, reading it, editing together packages; that was how local radio worked. But here was a chance to get back out there in the field once again, away from the studio.

Everyone was startled by the absence of planes over London that morning. Five airports serviced the city, including, to the north, Luton, to the east, Stansted and London City, and in the south, Gatwick. At Heathrow the planes land and take off every forty-five seconds, from five in the morning until midnight, and no one who lived in West London failed to be anything other than amazed by the effect of the planes stopping. Richmond, where

Harriet lived, was right there, just a few kilometers from the airport, right under the flight path.

Harriet was not good at recognizing professional opportunities when they came her way. She never noticed the door opening until after it had shut again. It began to happen when she was young and starting out in her career, and it happened when she returned to work after Jack was born; her chance departed before she noticed it had arrived. She had never intended to stay at the local radio news desk for all this time, but she had. And today the opportunity was right there in front of her. Harriet had done her research. This was *the* local story, and the station did not have enough reporters to cover it.

She grabbed her producer by the sleeve as he walked past her desk. Even that was a complete departure. "Let me do a story," she said. Steve looked down at her, almost wriggling with impatience.

He didn't speak, but she could see he was considering it.

"I'll go out west, toward Heathrow, right under the flight path. Onto the streets. Record the silence. Talk to people. See what they think."

Steve straightened his sleeve where she had rumpled it. "Take Barney," he said. "Just this once."

Barney was a sound engineer who, like Harriet, had got stuck in the studio, in his case behind the sound desk. He had a disabled wife at home, so he worked short days and had curtailed his ambitions in the same way that Harriet had curtailed her own after she had Jack. For

Barney this had worked out rather well, as the new technologies had eliminated the need for much of what in the
past had been necessary for sound recording. He'd kept
his radio job, while a lot of his old friends had had to
retrain.

They made a plan: after the lunchtime news, they'd
go out. They cackled together in the newsroom, full of
glee at the prospect of escape. Harriet noticed the younger
staff watching, and saw herself and Barney from their
point of view: middle-aged, wild-eyed, slightly deranged.
Pah, she thought, who cares?

The conversation with Barney left Harriet wound up,
so she went into the loo to calm down. She had a good
voice for radio, warm, sisterly, calm, confiding. She could
announce that one hundred people had died in a bomb
explosion, or thousands had died in floods, in exactly the
right tone, at exactly the right pace. But she had started
out in TV and now, she told herself, she was ready to
return to TV. She stood in front of the mirror and looked
at herself. Despite working in radio, she always tried to
look professional, unlike her colleagues who wore their
jeans and nubbly fleeces, old stretched cardigans and
faded hoodies, whether they were in front of the micro-
phone or not. Today she wore a smart jacket, nipped in at
the waist, flaring around the hips, over a summery dress,
heels. A chunky necklace, discreet but sparkly earrings, a
cocktail ring. She hauled her makeup out of her handbag
and touched up her foundation and her under-eye con-
cealer. She layered on the bronzer. Gave her straight hair

a brush. "I'm glad I didn't cut it," she said to the mirror. She felt a moment of pride at her appearance, but then . . . "Too old," she said. "I'm too fucking old." She applied her lipstick very carefully, to prevent it from seeping up into the cracks around her lips. "It's radio, Harriet. Local radio."

6

In Dubai, the building company that Yacub worked for went bust.

When he first arrived, he'd been shocked to discover that the labor camp's terms and conditions, to which he'd agreed in the recruiting office in Karachi, were meaningless. Not only was the salary lower than he'd been promised—instead of three thousand dirhams a month, he was paid seven hundred—but the workers' accommodation was not provided for free, and he was required to pay for his rent and food, leaving him with around two hundred dirhams a month. At that rate, it would take him years to earn back the fee he'd paid the recruiter in Karachi. The work was tough, mostly unskilled, loading and unloading materials, but Yacub worked hard and gained his foreman's trust, and after three months, his wage was raised to a thousand dirhams, with a promise of more to come. The story in the camp was that there had been an inspection, and the American company that was going to occupy the office building once it was finished was not happy about the workers' conditions.

"You were right, Yacub," said his boss. Imran was a Pakistani too, a fellow Swati, as tall and fair-skinned as Yacub was small and dark. He loved his mother and "football, not cricket," as he was fond of stating, "Manchester United." Imran hated the UAE, "a country," he said, "that will rape you and then ask you to pay for it," even though he was one of the people making money, one of the people making those beneath him pay for it. He was seated at the temporary office he set up in the camp courtyard on payday every month—a desk, a folding chair, a large sun umbrella, a cooler full of ice and cans of Diet Coke that he dispensed to the men he favored. "Terms and conditions, my son," he said, speaking their native Pashtun instead of Urdu, "it's all about terms and conditions."

Five months later, the company had gone bust, and Imran disappeared, along with his temporary office.

"So," Yacub's friend, Farhan, said, the first morning they stood in an impatient crowd waiting at the camp bus stop for a bus that, as the sun came up and the heat of the day rose, was clearly not coming, "the rumors are true."

Farhan was a boy from Lahore who'd abandoned a half-finished degree in dentistry when his father died. Despite his nearly middle-class origins, Farhan had thought it would be lucrative to spend a year working as a laborer in Dubai, sending money home to his widowed mother, but once there, he found himself as trapped as the lowliest Lahori streetsweeper. His partial degree meant he was able to practice rudimentary dentistry in the camp on his day off. However, he made little money this way, because his fellow laborers had little money with which to pay him. "But still," he'd say to Yacub, "an eye for an eye, a tooth for a hundred dirhams. Better than nothing."

"What are the rumors?" Yacub asked, keeping his voice low. Despite sharing a room with seven men who took every opportunity to exchange unfounded reports and outrageous gossip, Yacub was never in the loop, unable to pick out the real story from the broiling stream of misinformation that passed through the camp every evening.

"That's it," Farhan said.

"What do you mean?"

"We're bust. Shut down. The company has pulled out. And left all of us to rot."

Yacub stared down the road. Identical three-story blocks of the labor camp stretched as far as he could see. Ordinarily he'd have to pull a chador across his face to prevent the dust raised by the traffic from choking him. This morning there was no traffic. No dust either. Just the great crowd of mostly silent, waiting men.

"Have you got enough money for the airfare home?" Farhan asked.

Yacub felt his stomach turn over. He shook his head.

"Stupid question," said Farhan. "Me neither."

After they'd contemplated the empty road for a little longer, Farhan spoke up once again. "He has a sideline in girls."

"Who?"

"Imran."

"Girls?" Yacub frowned. One of the astonishing features of life in Dubai was the complete absence of women. Yacub could not recall the last time he'd spoken to a woman. He'd seen them, in cars that ran alongside the transit bus as it took him from the camp to the building site and in the distance near the big hotels where the road ran along the beach. But that was it.

At that moment, when Farhan said the word "girls," Yacub felt a homesickness for his sister, Raheela, that was so deep it was almost crippling. He blinked and tried not to think about her, about the journey they had made to Karachi after their father, then their mother had died. Now, he had come to Dubai in order to earn money to send home to her. Raheela remained in Karachi, in a domestic job in a good household; she sent him cheerful postcards covered with her tiny, careful handwriting. He wanted her to go to college, but she was becoming increasingly devout; the last time he saw her, she had covered herself entirely, even when they were alone.

"Our lovely Pakistani sisters and aunties work for Imran," Farhan continued. "The lighter-skinned, the better. Gulf girls are worth the most, of course, and Chinese girls the least, but our sisters do all right."

"How do you know all this?"

"Imran told me. If you would ever do as I ask and sit up late with us, you'd have figured out that what he's been drinking from that flask all day is whiskey. And when he's drunk, he likes to chat. I've learned many things this way."

"What do the girls do here?" As soon as he'd said it, Yacub wished he could unsay it.

Farhan looked at him. "They don't have to pay the recruitment fees. They just turn up, apparently. And *they* are the ones who are making real money here in Dubai. Well, them and Imran."

"Oh," said Yacub. He felt a bit sick.

"Anyway, Imran was always saying that it turned out his night job was much more lucrative than his day job. So that's what he's doing, I reckon."

"*Inshallah*," Yacub said.

Farhan laughed.

The sun was high now. Most of the other workers had given up waiting for the bus and gone back indoors.

That was December. By April 2010, it had been four months since they were last paid. And in the camp, the water and electricity had been turned off in February.

7

Michael was in New York for meetings at the headquarters of his firm. Because of the downturn, these business trips had become rare over the past two years, so Michael was pleased to be in the city. He liked New York, and he missed coming over regularly. He'd flown in on Wednesday, been in meetings Thursday and Friday, at company dinners every night, so it wasn't until he turned on the television in his hotel room on Saturday morning—oh, the pleasure of watching CNN in a hotel bedroom—that he saw the pictures of the ash cloud and watched the stories about people stranded around the world, unable to get home. It took him a while to realize that he was one of those people.

He had planned a day of shopping and wandering around the city before flying home to London that evening. He called the office assistant and asked her what she could do about rebooking his flight. "The ash will clear," he said, "the planes will be flying again by tonight." The girl laughed, and he was taken aback. Even so, he decided to proceed with his morning as though everything was normal. He always bought jeans when he was in New York, even though he never wore them at home, but his idea of himself as a jeans wearer persisted. He had a shelf in his closet where he kept them neatly folded, in chronological order, from oldest to newest, and, coincidentally, from smallest to largest.

Jack had discovered the jeans recently. "Jesus, Dad," he said, "what's that about?"

Michael looked at the pile and felt a bit ridiculous. "That's your inheritance, Son. Right there. Worth a fortune on eBay. Vintage."

"Fuck," he said now, not quite under his breath, when he realized his waist had expanded again. He was standing in the change room in his boxers and socks, shivering slightly. He asked the shop assistant to fetch him a larger size. Then his phone rang.

"There are no flights," said the girl. "I managed to get through—the airspace shutdown shows no signs of lifting. They do not advise going to the airport."

"Oh," said Michael.

"I also phoned your hotel. I'm afraid you'll have to check out, Mr. Smith. They're fully booked."

"Damn," said Michael.

"I've called a few other hotels in the city, but they're all full too. I'll keep trying, but Mr. Evans has said that if we have no luck, I'm to send a car to take you to his place in Westchester this afternoon."

Michael looked at the floor of the change room. Someone knocked and handed him a larger pair of jeans. The idea of spending even a single evening in the company of his American counterpart, Jeff Evans, in his Westchester home made Michael want to die. Spending social time with other actuaries was not his idea of fun.

"That's kind of Jeff," Michael said. "Please thank him for me." Michael paused. He stared at the wall of the change room. Where to go? What to do? Canada, he thought. Marina. "I'll go to Toronto. I've got a friend there."

"Oh yeah," said the young woman—Michael had no idea of her name—"I always forget you're Canadian."

He'd wait it out in Toronto. He'd go stay with Marina. His oldest friend, Marina. "Yes," he said. "I'll be fine. I'll take the train. Or a bus. Or I'll drive." The idea of flying anywhere was no longer appealing.

"Would you like me to look into that for you?"

"Okay," said Michael. "Thanks." He put his BlackBerry into the pocket of his jacket and put on the enormous jeans. They fit perfectly. As he stood in line to pay, a message came through on his phone with a new itinerary: the assistant had booked a train to Buffalo that afternoon, a hotel in Buffalo that night, and the train through to Toronto the following morning.

Michael was going home to Canada. He'd lived abroad for so long that the word alone—"Canada"—was enough to tip him into a warm pool of nostalgia. Canada. And Marina.

8

Emily's job as a television researcher kept her busy. The reality show market was as rapacious as always, and she had a knack for finding and persuading people to be filmed. She worked freelance, so she had to hustle for contracts, but she did all right. She was working on a new program about the fattest people in Britain; it had renewed her enthusiasm for cycling. Her dad had alternated between being thrilled by her success in what he saw as the high-pressure cutthroat world of factual television, and working hard to stifle his disapproval of the content she worked on. "Freak show," was his line. Part of her thought he was right, but it was a job, and she was good at it. She went back to work the day after her dad's funeral. Several of her colleagues were stranded abroad, so her boss needed her to come in.

Emily knew her father wasn't her birth father; she'd always known she was adopted. Her adoptive mother died when she was two years old, and she and her dad had been on their own since then. She'd wondered about her birth parents and from time to time had considered doing something to find them, but she'd always been secretly appalled by other people's birth-parent-quest tales, proud of her and her adoptive father's self-sufficiency. One of her first-ever jobs was on a show about birth siblings who'd grown up apart and who'd fallen in love with each other without knowing they were related—huge ratings hit. Her father had been dismayed by the program, but it enabled her to raise the subject of whether she should look for her own birth parent.

"Well," he'd said, "you'd have to go to social services and start the paperwork, I guess."

"There will be records, won't there?"

"Yes," he said. "You're allowed to request them—I believe the authorities will help you get in touch, if that's what you want." He cleared his throat and shifted in his seat. "You can probably do all that online these days."

"You don't want me to do this?" she asked.

He grimaced.

"Daddy," she said—she hadn't called him Daddy for a long time. She put her arms around him. He breathed into her hair.

That night, when she got home, she'd put "how to find your birth parents" into the search engine and clicked around the websites that came up. There were official forms to fill in. She opened one and began to input her details; she'd have to start from scratch—her father probably had her original birth certificate, but she didn't want to ask him for it. She got halfway through the form and stopped. Starting the process would lead somewhere. There would be an outcome. There would be consequences. Her birth parents, whoever they were, wherever they were, would be told she was looking for them. They would respond—either by denying her request or by agreeing to it. She had lived her twenty-four years of life without them. If she clicked on send, that would change.

She closed the browser.

When she told her almost boyfriend, Harvinder, that her father had died, he burst into tears over the phone. He cycled straight over to see her, though she had asked him not to, and when she opened the door, he burst into tears once again. She couldn't hide her annoyance; she stuck both her hands into the pouch of her hoodie and shuffled into the kitchen, leaving him to follow. She stood by the counter, clutching her cup of tea.

"He was so sweet, your dad," Harv said.

"Sweet" made him sound like an old man. He was not an old man. "He thought you were a plonker," Emily said. "He thought I was too good for you. He used to call you a Hoxton hipster manqué."

Harv laughed. "That's so sweet, though, can't you see? All good dads think that about their daughters' boyfriends."

"You're not really my boyfriend, Harv, are you." When Emily thought back to this conversation later, she blamed her cold, hard frankness on her father's death. "You like having a 'girlfriend,'" she said, "but really, you're gay."

Harv looked at her, shook his head and gave a small shrug, as though he'd been accused of this many times. "You're not yourself," he said. "You can say whatever you want to me. I'm here for you." He teared up once again. "You're an orphan now, Em."

She put her tea down on the counter. An orphan. This hadn't occurred to her. An only child, both parents gone. Her throat tightened. She didn't want to cry in front of Harv. What was the use of an almost boyfriend if you couldn't cry on his shoulder? "Thanks for coming round, Harv. That'll be all, though," she said.

"I'm going to go get us something to eat. You shouldn't be on your own. I'll be back in half an hour."

"No," she said. "Time to go. Don't come back."

He looked at her sharply, hearing the tone in her voice. "Tomorrow, then?"

She shook her head. "No. We're done here." She left the kitchen and opened the front door of the flat.

He followed her. "You're not yourself. I'll call you."

She shook her head, no, and didn't speak.

9

That night, Harriet got back from work late once again. At lunch she had sat outside with her sandwich, looking up into the blue sky. Cloudless days were unusual in London and, while the ash cloud covered Europe, these lovely clear days were spooky. She'd read the reports and looked at the satellite photos and knew that, bizarrely, the ash cloud wasn't visible in London, but even so, if she stared hard enough, would she be able to see the air up high limned with tiny shards of ice? Was the ash cloud actually visible from anywhere other than outer space? As she walked down the street from the train station, the night sky was silent; who would have predicted that the most compelling result of the end of aviation would be the silence? It was both alarming and soothing. Harriet couldn't decide whether it was idyllic or apocalyptic. This is what it must have felt like in the past, before the twentieth century really got going, when the sky was full of weather and stars, weather and stars only.

When she opened the front door, the house was silent too. Jack's bedroom door was firmly shut, no music emanating; he must be asleep already. Michael was stuck in New York. Harriet still hadn't managed to speak to him, but she wasn't worried. She knew that his company would take care of him and he'd get home, eventually. The house was hers and hers alone, and while tonight she thought this was a blissful novelty, it was also a glimpse of what it might be like in a few years' time after Jack left home. She didn't like the idea of an empty house. Maybe she and Michael should have had more children. The idea that we build new families through our networks of friends hadn't really worked out; we are on our own, mostly. And she hadn't seen her own parents in years.

She made herself a cup of herbal tea and drank it in the bath with the radio on, volume on low. Then she got into bed and turned on her tablet.

It had first occurred to Harriet to look for Emily online a few years ago. She had been in the kitchen, trying to get Jack off the games console so they could eat, when it came to her—boom: Emily was probably on Facebook.

Wherever she was, she must be on Facebook—unless she'd been kidnapped and taken to North Korea. Everyone was on Facebook, or at least everyone Emily's age. Harriet could follow her. Harriet could be her "friend."

She abandoned trying to get Jack to come to the dinner table. She turned on her computer, opened up her account, and put in Emily's name. A whole host of people with the same name appeared on her screen. She'd have to work through them and figure out which was the right girl. She'd have to open a new account, one that made her look young and groovy, someone Emily could friend without thinking about it much: "Crazeeharree." By the next day Harriet had not only found Emily but the friend request had been successful. As simple as that. We're "friends," Harriet thought. Her hands were shaking. Jack had his headphones on but, even so, Harriet turned up the volume on the radio. She opened the door to the little room at the back of the kitchen, where they stored all their useless and unwanted stuff, went inside, closed the door, and screamed. Then she went back into the kitchen, turned the radio down, and resumed cooking.

Later that night, once she was sure Jack was asleep, Harriet returned to her computer. She took her time navigating to Emily's page, like she was opening a door to spy on someone in the next room, trying to prevent the hinges from creaking. She clicked on the link and stopped, afraid to click any further, as though Emily would be able to tell that she was there. She made sure her chat facility was turned off and proceeded to move around Emily's pages stealthily. Friends. Info. Her favorite things. It was all there.

It was a shock to see her. Harriet had not seen her— not a single photograph, and of course not in the flesh either—since all those years ago. Here she was, a grown woman, with long, silky dark brown hair and fashionable spectacles and a fondness for scoop-neck T-shirts, chunky necklaces and bracelets. Here she was, in a parade of photographs, with her friends, two girls, three girls, four girls and five boys, crammed together, smiling wildly, holding bottles of beer, in hats, in bikini tops, in bars, in fancy dress on outings, dozens and dozens of digital images, as though Emily's life was an endless party, documented, posted, reposted, tagged, commented on, shared, liked. Harriet stared at the photographs, hoping for clues about Emily, beyond the information posted on her pages. Who was she?

And now, in bed with her tablet at the end of a long day, Harriet watched her, like a ghost stalker, a quiet, persistent presence, hovering in the ether. She'd been following her online for several years, but she still didn't really know what Emily was like. Emily's friends had posted multiple new messages on her page, and Harriet realized with a shock that Emily's adoptive father had recently died. She flicked back and forth between the posts. She could send her a message. It would be easy, here, by herself in front of the computer. "Hey Emily," she could post, "it's me." She'd thought about doing this many times, but the story she had to tell was too complex, too convoluted and confusing. She'd never told the story, not to Michael, not to Jack. Only the people who were present at that time knew what had happened, and she'd lost touch with everyone.

Harriet used the touchscreen to enlarge the most recent photo of Emily. It was painful to look at her, but she'd got used to it, and now it would be more painful not to look. What can I do to help her through this? What can I say, without fucking up everything? Will she want to know me? When the day comes and she learns the true story, will she turn away?

10

"What do you think?"

Young black woman, smartly dressed: "Oh, it's amazing, isn't it? The sky—it's like we've arrived in the future or something."

"What about you, sir?"

Older Asian man, in a suit: "My fifteen-year-old daughter is in the South of France on a language exchange. How on earth am I supposed to get her home? It's not like she can hire a car and drive to Calais."

Polish man, thirty-something: "I'm stuck here! I came over to visit my brother. He works at Heathrow, so he now has some extra time to see me, which is good. But London is so expensive. If I have to stay much longer, I'll have to get a job, like all the other Polish people!"

"And you?"

Older white woman: "I'm loving it. My husband is stranded in Norway, but he's with friends, so he's okay. I love the quiet. It's so peaceful. It would be brilliant if Richmond was like this all the time."

The interviews were going well; it had been a good idea to come to this part of town, far west, close to Heathrow. Everyone on the high street was in a curiously good mood, despite their stories of children, partners, and colleagues stranded. It was as though the air had cleared finally after a long deluge.

Pensioner, with a walking frame: "I never realized before that the sky is so full of noise. I know that we see and hear and feel the planes most days, but I'm amazed at how accustomed I'd become. I'd be happy if the planes never returned." Barney videoed the interviews at the same time as recording the sound. After they'd amassed a fair amount of material, Harriet suggested they head over to Richmond Park to record the lack of noise.

Barney laughed. "That'll make good radio."

"No, come on," Harriet said, "you'll see. It's a good idea."

Because the Easter school holidays were still on, the road traffic was very light. In fact, the whole of London felt depopulated. In the park they walked until they found a copse for Harriet to stand in. The sun was shining and the daffodils were out. The trees had that tentative, early-spring look, caught between leaf and blossom. A large flock of bright green West London parakeets settled in one of the oaks. Barney turned his camera on, and what they expected to be silence was, of course, full of sound—birds, the light breeze in the leaves and grass, in the distance a dog barking, a car passing. Harriet found it hard not to smile. She spread her arms and looked up into the sky, which was completely, solidly blue.

"No jet streams," she said. "Not a single jet stream."

Back in the studio, they cut together the piece, managing to persuade Steve to give them five minutes instead of the two he'd said he wanted. They edited a video version as well, to post on the station website.

"This will make you a star, Harriet," Barney said.

Harriet snorted. "Middle-Aged Woman Happy in Park."

The piece went out on the five o'clock news. Harriet handled the links and read the news, as always. The presenter, Josh, in his avuncular local radio voice said, "And now, for a piece on the effect of the ash cloud beneath the flight path into Heathrow, over to our very own newsreader, Harriet Smith." Harriet and Barney stood up and applauded each other as the package went live.

11

When it first sank in that his father was stranded across the Atlantic, Jack was worried. On the news, they talked about the ash cloud dispersing and blowing away. But the volcano kept erupting, spewing clouds of smoke and ice into the atmosphere: it had been erupting continuously for days, and the cloud continued to spread and thicken. There was talk of a second volcano beginning to rumble: it turned out that Iceland was heaving with active volcanoes. Online there were rumors about test planes flying into the cloud and being forced to make emergency landings, the millions of tiny shards of ice in the cloud attacking the engines, stripping the paint off the fuselage. Jack's father was stuck and Jack had no idea when he might see him again.

Despite all this, or maybe because of it, Jack felt that his moment had arrived. He wasn't sure why. Probably a hormone-induced fantasy—one among many. Not only was his father stranded across the Atlantic Ocean but his mother was at work for longer hours than normal, from before Jack got up to after he'd retreated to his room at night. He was in his preferred state, unsupervised, on holiday, free to hang out with whoever he wanted, free to go wherever he felt like. School was due to start again tomorrow, and that made this final weekend all the sweeter.

Jack wanted to live his life. That's one of the bad things about being a kid: you aren't allowed to live your life. Well, today, he would.

Jack's mother kept leaving money on the kitchen counter for him to buy takeaway, but he resisted and stuck to eating white bread with chocolate spread, with the occasional orange thrown in to keep him healthy. Instead of buying food, he used the money to buy draw. He gave the money to Ruby, so she could give it to her brother, who would then give the stuff to Ruby, so she could give it to Jack. Overnight, he had become popular. People wanted to hang out with him. Ruby wanted to hang out with him.

Jack was crap at rolling spliffs so Ruby did it, or sometimes Frank, though he was worse at it but better at pretending he knew what he was doing. At Dukes, one of the big mums, shepherding a herd of toddlers, chased Jack and his friends away from the children's playground where they'd been hanging around the swings smoking, so they flopped down at the other end of the green by the river. It was sunny—the whole of April had been sunny. Jack couldn't remember ever experiencing such a sunny month. And the sky, well, while they tried to pretend smoking weed had no novelty, was nothing out of the ordinary, they allowed themselves to continue to marvel at the clean plane-less sky.

Jack felt wavy straightaway. Before, when he'd had the odd puff here or there off one of Ruby's tiny, tightly rolled spliffs, he didn't feel much at all—his feet would get a bit heavy, and he'd get the beginnings of a headache. It wasn't like with beer where a single can made him feel hilarious. This was an altogether stranger feeling.

They lay in a row on the grass holding hands—Frank, Abdul, Dore, Ruby, and Jack—like those paper doll cutouts they used to make in primary school. Somebody's dog, off its leash, came running past and sniffed them all over. They didn't mind. The sky was unbelievably blue.

"We need a party, man," said Frank, "we need to go to a party."

"Nobody has parties on Sunday afternoon, Frank," said Abdul. "Except your parents."

They all laughed, except they were too lethargic to laugh out loud, so they laughed on the inside. Jack could feel Ruby giggling beside him. Frank's parents were famous for their Sunday afternoon barbecues where Frank's large extended family would gather and get drunk. Invitations were coveted by Frank's friends because of the availability of booze once the adults had had too much to notice.

"No party today," said Frank. "My parents have taken a vow of chastity—no, that's not right, what is it?—abstinence. Uncle Ned had an epileptic fit and the doctor told him he's an alcoholic. So everyone's having a go at not drinking."

"Wow," said Ruby. "How long will that last?"

"Till the doctor apologizes or something."

"I don't know that I'd want to go to one of those barbecues if they aren't drinking," said Abdul. "It would be weird."

"I know. My mum poured my dad's whiskey down the sink. He stood there nodding and sighing. I thought they were going to cry."

Everyone was quiet again. Jack had lost the power of speech. He couldn't believe that school was starting again the next day. He wanted to prolong this feeling. He wondered if it was possible to stay wavy permanently.

"There's a party next Friday," said Ruby. "At David McDonald's house."

David McDonald was much older, at least seventeen, maybe even eighteen. He was famous for being a Big Man at school. He'd never speak to a lowly fourteen-year-old like Jack. But everybody talked to Ruby.

"Can you get us in?" asked Frank.

"I can try," Ruby said.

12

On Sunday, Harriet spent a chunk of time with Barney at Heathrow Airport. They had to use their press passes to get in; the police were denying access to anyone other than press and airport employees. Heathrow is a vast conglomeration of five terminals, a self-contained world of shopping, catering, and security. "Like life itself," Barney said as they drove from terminal to terminal, "you check in, you eat, you shop, you depart."

Except now no one was departing, or arriving; no planes had landed since Thursday. Instead the airport was functioning as a displaced persons camp, the DPs all the non-UK nationals who had nowhere else to go, no money to find other routes home, no money to book into hotels. The airport had become their home. Each terminal had its own forecourt tent city, and the seating areas were packed with people trying to sleep, people who hadn't slept for days. They were stretched out on top of tables and benches, beneath tables and benches. Harriet saw one family who had turned an airport mobility transport vehicle into their temporary home. In the glossy and sleek new building of Terminal 5, the departure and arrival boards were entirely blank. The taxi ranks were vacant. Everyone had given up shouting. A lone cleaner cleaned. A large man stretched out across several seats moaned loudly. Somewhere in the sleepless crowd, a baby was crying.

Harriet still hadn't spoken to Michael, but he'd emailed her several times on Saturday night from his hotel in Buffalo. The time difference and Harriet's work schedule made it hard for her to find the right moment to call, and by the time she got home at night, sorted out Jack, made something to eat, cleared away Jack's debris, she was so tired she forgot about Michael. At least Jack would be back at school on Monday, not that Harriet worried about him when he was out with his friends. She knew he was a good boy. She told herself she trusted him, when what she really meant was that she hoped he was all right, he had to be all right. She needed to work. She was in the middle of grabbing her opportunity. It was an unfamiliar maneuver, and she needed both hands free.

It was hard to see how it would end: the wind needed to change direction, the volcano needed to stop erupting. The enormous inconvenience of it all was awesome to behold—but it was just that, an enormous inconvenience. No lives had been lost. No one had been blown up. No one had been gunned down. A volcano was erupting, and its ash cloud was drifting over Europe, and there was nothing anyone could do about it. The airlines had begun to agitate for changes to the safety regulations. The news was full of stories about desperate people hiring taxis at great expense to drive across Europe, passenger ships to and from New York were booked out, and the government was planning to deploy the navy to repatriate stranded Brits. In his emails Michael sounded calm; he was going to Toronto to wait it out. Going to Toronto seemed like a good idea; he could stay with his old friend Marina. It would be good for him to spend some time in Canada. They hadn't been to Vancouver, where he'd grown up, for years, but Harriet knew he liked Toronto. Harriet had never met Marina. It wasn't like Michael to stay with a friend. But these were exceptional circumstances, exceptional times. Harriet wondered when he'd be able to come home. But she couldn't let herself worry about that, not yet.

Harriet would go see Mallory Flynn. Harriet had known Mallory since they were first starting out. Mallory had gone on to greater things: hers was one of those career paths that followed a proper trajectory, taking off and achieving ever-greater heights. Unlike Harriet's. She'd go see Mallory and talk about work. Talk about moving on from local radio, back into—back into what? Harriet wasn't sure. But once things calmed down at work, that's what she'd do. She'd go have a drink with Mallory. She'd call in a favor. Except Mallory didn't owe her any favors. Still, they had known each other a long time, and that had to count for something.

13

Michael phoned Marina from Buffalo on Saturday night.

When she picked up the receiver, she was in the middle of a coughing fit, so he held on while she got it under control. "Hello?" she said, eventually.

"Hello, Marina," he said, "it's Michael."

No reply. He could hear her swallowing heavily, still choking a bit.

"Michael Smith," he said.

"I know who you are!" She sounded as though she was half-strangled. "Just give me a minute."

"Okay," he said. He leaned back against the pillows on the hotel bed. A tune came into his head. He hummed a bit under his breath, then broke out singing: "London calling . . ." He even did Joe Strummer's yelp.

"Idiot," Marina said into the phone. She had her voice back. Unmistakably Marina, low and silky. They saw the Clash together in Vancouver in 1979. The Commodore Ballroom. The crowd was so overexcited and violent that the band stopped playing after four songs. Marina was a proper punk, or at least as proper a punk as possible for an Iranian girl in as nonpunk a place as Vancouver. Even then Michael knew the torn T-shirt he was wearing made him look like he was going to grow up to be an actuary, like someone who tore his T-shirt accidentally and hadn't had time to go home and change.

"I'm coming to town," he said.

"How? No planes across the Atlantic."

"The train! We Europeans often travel by train."

She sighed. Michael could tell he was annoying her already.

"I was stranded in New York. Nowhere to stay. So I thought I'd come to Toronto. To see you."

"Are you still a banker?"

She knew what he did, but they liked to annoy each other.

"Yes," he said, "still a fat cat. Though now I actually am kind of fat. Put on a bit of weight in the last couple of years—just to prepare you, so the shock of seeing me doesn't kill you."

"You were always too skinny."

It was one of the great things about having friends who knew you when you were young: when they picture you they see what you looked like when you were eighteen, not what you look like now that you're pushing fifty. That's why those Facebook reunions of high school sweethearts are so common: these people take one look at each other and the years of poor diet, no exercise, and too much television fall away. But Michael knew Marina would never be so soft. He was sure her hard edges were sharpening with age.

"You need a place to stay."

"I don't know," he said, "haven't looked into it yet."

"The hotels in Toronto are as full as the hotels in New York," she said. "There's a lot of gouging going on, apparently, rooms tripling in price. You'll come and stay with me. You never have. It's about time."

He gave her his arrival time and Marina said she'd meet him.

"I'll be the fat guy in a suit," he said.

She laughed. Marina. Michael's first girlfriend.

After he left Vancouver, they stayed in touch via ironic postcards, Michael sending royal family memorabilia for the most part, Marina specializing in Canadiana—the Mountie on his horse, the stuffed black bear on his hind legs outside the tourist shop. They knew before they started dating that their relationship was time-limited; Michael had already been accepted at the London School of Economics. As a result, their relationship had an unnatural natural ease to it, a live-for-today clarity. The advent of email had revived their correspondence just at the point it was beginning to fade away, and they'd kept up sporadic contact that way. Michael was a Facebook refusenik; no amount of nudging and poking and requesting would make him change his mind. But he used to travel to Toronto for business fairly regularly before the crash, and he would see Marina whenever he was in town; they'd have dinner together somewhere smart and new. Marina always knew about the next big thing before it became the next big thing, by which time she'd have moved on to the one after that. She'd worked as an interior stylist for a home decor magazine for many years, before finding an investor and opening her own store. Furniture, lamps, a select range of luxurious clothes made for lounging on the furniture lit by the lamps, and an even more select range of jewelry with a tasteful Persian influence. No carpets. Years before, she had extricated herself—painfully—from her father's Vancouver business to go to art school in Toronto, and she wasn't going anywhere near Persian carpets. You couldn't buy anything in her shop for less than a couple of months' worth of mortgage payments. Yorkville, of course—the funky bit, where the streets are narrow and the old houses have been transformed into shops and galleries.

At the train station Michael spotted her immediately: long black wildly curly hair, tall and straight-backed and a little forbidding in her layers of black clothes and startling jewelry. She was always lightly tanned, even in the depths of winter; she claimed it was her Eastern genes. She hadn't gone leathery like some women do; instead she looked bronzed, as though a sculptor had made a cast of her and she'd left her old body behind in the studio.

It took her a while to spot Michael on the platform as he walked toward her. But then she smiled, and her smile tore through his layers of aging flesh until he felt as though she found the real him, the one she wanted to see. She embraced him and gave him a big kiss.

"Fatty!" she said.

"Porker," Michael replied. "I think you'll find they call me Mr. Fatty Porker down at the bank."

"Dick Schwein!" she shrieked. They'd had a thing for

swearing at each other in mock German, Michael couldn't remember why.

"Mr. Dick Schwein," Michael said.

Marina lived alone in the big house that she and her husband, Stewart, had bought back in the '90s, an old house for Toronto, early twentieth century, with hardwood floors and high molded ceilings. It had been renovated so thoroughly that the original house was mainly a genetic memory, everything precision engineered for the utmost in comfort in the best possible taste. It was a machine for living, with wide doors that opened onto big rooms full of long couches, vast, pristine countertops in the kitchen, a warm rosewood table in the eating area, bathrooms that were almost too perfect to use. She showed him to his room, and when he put down his suitcase, all he could think was that it looked far too battered and grubby. In all the years that they had kept in touch, he had never stayed with her, not in Vancouver when she still lived there with her parents, not after she moved to Toronto to go to university. She had never been to London. They had slept together for the last time when they were eighteen.

"You fancy a margarita at the Boulevard Café?" she asked. "I made a dinner reservation at a new place for later."

"Are you single these days?" Michael asked.

She laughed and indicated the perfect room in which they stood. "I've got a new husband, a dog, and a couple of kids stashed away somewhere," she said, "but I like to keep things neat."

"Stewart was a neat freak," Michael said. He hadn't known Stewart well, but his funeral had coincided with a trip to Toronto in 2004, so he'd attended. It was a big gathering at St. James' Cathedral: Stewart had been the editor of the magazine where Marina had worked, and he was well known and well liked in media circles. It was an icy February day and the stylish crowd were dressed in sleek black wool coats, with a preponderance of clunky black spectacles and neat little hats. The women wore brooches; the men had stylish facial hair. People dress to charm and amuse in Toronto in a way that no one would ever dream of in London, Michael thought. On that day, for the first and only time in her life, Marina was pale.

"People used to say that Stewart was the neat freak, but it turns out that, all along, it was me."

"Let me buy you a margarita," Michael said.

"Fine with me, Dick Schwein," Marina said, and as she slipped her arm through his, her hair brushed against his cheek. It felt right to be there with her while the sky out over the Atlantic had fallen silent. Michael had no doubt that the planes would fly again before too long. But if he was going to be stranded anywhere, it was meant to be here, in Toronto, with Marina.

14

The weekend after her father's funeral, Emily took herself out for a long cycle ride along the Thames. He'd been dead for ten days. Ten days. She'd done the funeral. She'd gone back to work—what else could she do? She'd convinced Harv to stop calling. There was no one to stay up with all night, wailing. She had to get on with life. She had no other family—well, that wasn't completely true. Now that her father was gone, she could fill in that birth parent search form without worrying about hurting him.

The weather was glorious but the empty sky unnerved her, made her feel cut off, as though she'd lost contact with the world as well as her dad. She'd lived in Richmond for several years—North Sheen, really—and while it was a long way from the center of town, she liked its leafy suburban feel and its proximity to the river. She'd have to deal at some point with her father's house—he hadn't bought it, a council tenant all his life—but not yet. She'd tidy up her own life first. She pushed herself to cycle hard, as though the exertion and the sunshine would clear her mind. The wind made her eyes tear up, and she had to stop and get off her bike and sit on a bench because she couldn't see.

After a while her eyes stopped leaking. She got out her phone. She'd continued to receive lots of texts and emails and messages from her friends, and she went through the most recent ones now. She accepted an invitation to meet friends for drinks on the following weekend, thinking she'd better at least pretend to be alive, though she knew she'd cancel. She opened up Facebook. Harvinder had been posting photos of her and emoting all over the place about their breakup and her dad. She unfriended him. She opened up her list of friends and began unfriending systematically: people she didn't like, people who were friends of friends she'd never met, people she had no idea who they were. Through the *A*'s and the *B*'s, then on to the *C*'s. Crazeeharree. She paused. Who the fuck was that? Crazeeharree—soon to be deleted. Emily paused again. She'd take another look at this person's page first.

She opened it up. Odd. Only a handful of friends, most of whom were Emily's friends too. Female. No photos, apart from Emily's own, reposted without comment.

A shiver ran from the phone's screen through her body. I don't need to contact social services. I don't need to register with find-your-birth-parents online. There she is, right in front of me: Crazeeharree. Female.

Emily stood up from the bench so quickly, she almost fell over. She got on her bike. She needed to get home as fast as possible.

15

On Tuesday night Harriet got home from work a bit earlier, after nine. The studio was still missing half its staff, technicians, reporters, presenters; the people who'd been unable to get home last week continued to be unable to get home this week, same as Michael, who was still in Toronto. Harriet had done double shifts since Thursday and was tired.

Earlier that day, her boss had paid her the biggest compliment in his tiny arsenal of praise: "Well done," he said.

Harriet saw her opportunity. "I'd like you to call in a few favors on my behalf," she said.

Steve looked at her blankly. He was even more tired than her.

"I want to continue reporting—I want more of this kind of work."

He scratched his head and yawned. "You're a bit old for any of the training schemes."

Her mouth dropped open and her eyes went wide.

"I'm just saying, Harriet, you're not exactly fresh blood."

"I don't need any training, Steve. I've had training up the hoo-haa. I want the work." She did not attempt to curb the anger in her voice.

Steve held up one hand: stop. "Okay, okay—I'll have a think."

Harriet knew *have a think* meant *do nothing*. "I'd like you to send a recommendation to Mallory Flynn."

"Flynn? Television?"

"Yes. I know you know her. I know her too—from back in the day. I want you to send a recommendation to her and I'll follow it up myself."

"A recommendation?"

"Yes, Steve." Harriet knew the nagging tone she used when she was telling Jack to do his homework had crept into her voice, but she allowed it. "A recommendation. I'll write it for you, if you like. I've got all these pieces I've filed in the past week to show. Video as well as radio. You'll only have to okay it. Simple. Then it's out of your hands."

Steve looked at her. "Have we met before?" he asked. "I'm Steve."

"It's the ash cloud," she said. "New horizons."

"I'm nodding like I understand what you're talking about," said Steve.

She'd meet with Mallory. There was a general election around the corner. News coverage would increase exponentially for that event, and everyone who was anyone would be working that night. She'd offer up her expertise; she'd get herself back into the mainstream. Away from local radio. Back into television news, where she'd been before she met Michael, before she'd had Jack. On television, reporting.

———

Jack was lying on the sofa with the television on, asleep. Harriet could see he was drooling slightly. The carpet between the sofa and the coffee table had an asymmetrical layer of broken crisps ground into it. She spotted his backpack by the front door. He'd eaten the sandwiches she'd made him for lunch. He'd even got out his home-work—Harriet could see it on the coffee table amid the dirty glasses and games controllers. In the kitchen, she put a frozen meat pie into the oven and began to clear the dishes. She'd wake him when it was ready.

She turned on her computer and clicked on the BBC's live news feed. All day they'd been reporting that negoti-ations over lifting the flight ban were nearing completion. She made a salad and was sitting at the counter, waiting for the pie to be ready, propping up her heavy head with both hands, when the announcement came. Heathrow was reopening. At 10 p.m. the planes would start flying again. The first flight to take off was heading for Vancouver, Canada. Harriet pictured the airport waking, the depar-ture boards blinking back to life. She thought of Michael. She picked up the phone and dialed his BlackBerry, and left a message when he didn't reply. God knows how long it would take him to find a seat on a flight back to London.

It was peculiar—Michael had been gone less than two weeks, but it felt like much longer. There was a lot to tell him. He'd be pleased. She went to wake Jack. The pie was ready.

16

Jack didn't mind that school had started again. It was always good to see his friends, and classes didn't really get in the way of socializing. He'd found his first year in the school terrifying, what with the massive scary boys and shrieking terrifying girls in the playground, and so he hung out mostly with his old friends from primary school. Primary school was a doddle compared to secondary. His primary school was small and sweet, with lovely colorful classrooms and cuddly teachers, and awards for good behavior that hardly anyone got because everyone was good pretty much all of the time. Moving to secondary school had been traumatic. Jack felt as though he'd stolen a loaf of bread and been sent on convict transport to Australia. The school was a wild frontier, and he'd spent most of year seven worrying someone was going to kill him.

But he survived, and then in year eight he began to make new friends and find his way. It stopped bugging him that the big boys teased him for being middle-class. They tried calling him Smoked Salmon because his mum sent him to school with smoked salmon and cream cheese sandwiches instead of—what? Jack didn't know, chips in a white roll? Luckily, the nickname didn't stick. It was a crap nickname, and he liked the sandwiches his mother made. Once he began to grow, everything got easier. It's a simple truth that all it takes to intimidate a bully is a few inches of extra height.

Now, in year nine, Jack was fully acclimatized. He had learned the lingo. He didn't look confused when someone said "Wa'gwan" instead of "What's going on?" He'd learned to walk with his school trousers hanging off his butt. He knew when it was safe to go into the loos.

The first week back after the Easter holidays, he and his friends got into a nice routine of hanging out together after school. Jack's mum was still working much longer hours than normal and his dad was still stuck in Toronto. Half the teachers were stranded wherever they'd gone for their holidays, and a good chunk of the student body was absent as well. On Wednesday after school, Jack and his friends headed over to the local park. He produced his bag of draw, and they smoked a couple of spliffs and slipped into their cotton-wrapped world. They had the best conversations about everything. The sun shone and it was warm.

Everyone was lying on the grass, except Dore, who was on a swing. He was kicking his legs out hard, swinging higher and higher, when a plane passed overhead, lower than usual.

"I loved the empty sky," Ruby said. "I loved the silence." Her family lived farther west toward the airport, their house wedged beneath the flight path.

"It was too strange," Jack said. "I prefer it this way."

"Why?"

"The noise, the way the planes fly so low—I like knowing I could get on one and fly away. Besides, my dad can come home now."

"Well, I don't like it," said Ruby. "Our house shakes."

"Hey!" shouted Frank. When Frank got a bit wavy he'd automatically start shouting, as though smoking made him deaf. "What about David McDonald's party on Friday? Are we going?"

They looked at Ruby expectantly.

"I'll do my best," she said, and she gave a little shrug that made Jack want to hug her. But he did not.

17

Yacub was next in line in the queue at the water pipe when he saw the girls go by. There were six or seven of them, in a white stretch Mercedes limo, with the black-tinted windows rolled down. The limo drove past slowly, and the girls were laughing and chatting. He guessed they were Pakistani, he could hear last year's big Javed Bashir song blaring through the window. The men in the queue stared, even the man at the pipe looked away from his task, spilling water on the bone-dry ground. Then the limo turned a corner and was gone.

In the labor camp, the days trickled by in a sweat-soaked haze. Yacub tried to stay busy to stop himself from losing his grip—all around him, men were losing their grip. There'd been no electricity for months and the sewage truck had stopped coming. The only functioning standing pipe in the camp was about half a kilometer away from his building, so Yacub was among the small contingent who went to fetch water regularly. The population of the camp had declined fairly rapidly, by about a third, in the first month after the building company collapsed, as those who could afford to had left and a lucky few found other work. Because Imran, their foreman, had disappeared straightaway, none of the Pakistanis

Yacub knew had been able to find work—no referee, no references—and many of the building projects in Dubai had ground to a halt. After that first rush of departures, the population of the camp had leveled out: there were about one thousand men stranded now, with no way of leaving, mainly Indians, but Pakistanis, Bengalis, and a few Sri Lankans too. Many spent all day every day lying on their bunks. Yacub kept himself busy, helping out, organizing.

Early on, local shopkeepers had begun to extend lines of credit to the abandoned workers even though they must have known they stood a good chance of never being paid. Yacub was not among the delegation who visited the shops regularly, he couldn't face that, but he was happy to haul water and to forage for fuel for the make-shift ovens in the communal kitchen. He was among the regular delegation to the Pakistani Workers' Council offices, though those visits entailed a long dusty walk of several hours. Once there, he'd stand in the queue for a few hours more, before being told there was nothing they could do to help. Back at the camp they'd agreed to keep the visits up to make sure they were not forgotten. There were persistent rumors that the government of Pakistan was going to help the workers go home, but Yacub didn't believe them. Occasionally, the council distributed food for the men to carry back to the camp.

Yacub filled the two big plastic water vessels while the song "Aj Latha Naeeo" played in his head. He used to listen to music with Farhan on his friend's MP3 player.

Farhan guarded that MP3 player as though it was a bar of gold, but sometimes he'd allow Yacub to use one of the earbuds so they could listen together. Farhan had been one of the first to leave the camp after Imran failed to show up on payday. "You should leave now," he'd said to Yacub.

"Where are you going to go?"

"I have no idea," Farhan said, "but I'm not staying here."

The men behind him in the queue were talking about the burning ash cloud that had engulfed Europe, joking that at last the infidels were being punished. Yacub didn't believe a word of that either. He made his way back to his building, and as he drew nearer he could hear the music from the limo welling up once again. To his amazement, the car was parked in the courtyard of his building. The courtyard was packed with men; everyone had got up off their bunks and come out to see what was going on. They hung back from the car as though they were slightly afraid or suspicious of what might be inside. The windows were rolled up tight now so no one could see into the car; music—muffled but still very loud—was making both the car and the courtyard shake. The men stood and stared, and the white limousine vibrated.

As Yacub put down the water vessels, the man standing next to him said, "Can it be real?"

Before Yacub could reply, the music stopped. No one moved. The car's passenger doors opened and women spilled out. They were Pakistani girls, and they were dressed beautifully in cotton and linen shalwar kameez, blues and yellows and white and greens and pinks, patterns and stripes and solid blocks of color, lighting up the grimy, stinking courtyard. They placed their hands together and said hello, each one looking as embarrassed as the next. The men pushed back, pressing themselves farther away from the car and its women, as if to get too close would make this mirage disappear. The women turned toward the car as though to climb back inside, and a collective groan of disappointment went up from the crowd. But they were only doing what they had come to do; the women began to haul boxes and crates of food out of the car.

Ten minutes later, the car was emptied and the great pile of donated food supplies was stacked carefully against a wall. Hardly a word had been exchanged between the women and the men of the camp, until Bashir, one of the eldest, spoke up. "Thank you, dear daughters," he said. The women smiled in return and a wave of yearning passed through the men. Yacub thought of his sister; he'd been unable to afford to reply to her letters and they'd stopped arriving a couple of months before.

Imran emerged from the limo, a murky creature climbing out of the depths. He blinked hard in the unrelenting sunshine. He was dressed like an Emirati, in a white robe, his head covered. He spread his arms wide, a great leader come to greet his adoring people. Yacub felt the crowd draw back once again. He could feel his companions' anger as plainly as he felt the heat of the day; they were preparing to retaliate. Without thinking, Yacub rushed forward. He grabbed Imran's arm and said, "You better leave." He felt the crowd behind him.

"Why?" Imran asked. He was indignant. "Look what my girls have brought you!"

At that, the men surged forward. "Get in the car!" shouted Yacub. Somebody pushed Imran; someone else grabbed his sleeve, and when Imran tried to turn away, the cloth tore. He gave an undignified squawk and ducked into the limo, pulling Yacub with him, leaving the girls to follow behind. They piled in, slamming the doors, breathless. As the driver backed the limo out of the courtyard, the men closest to the car slammed their fists against the roof. Others pulled off their shoes and threw them, hitting the car, thunk, thunk, thunk. The driver accelerated backward. The men hurried out of the way, shouting and cursing. Yacub braced himself against the seat. The limo turned around and barreled up the roadway, air conditioning blasting.

Yacub was at the very back of the limo on the curved seat next to Imran. The girls lined the padded bench that ran the length of the car. Imran punched the buttons of the sound system overhead, turning the volume of the music back up. The girls were all talking at once, pulling off their dupattas, fanning away the heat with their scarves. Yacub, attempting not to stare, turned to Imran, who said, "Not very grateful, are they?"

"You owe us a lot of money," Yacub replied.

"Pah! Not my problem," said Imran. "The hotels are packed with European businessmen who can't go home because of the bloody volcano. Business is great. Right, girls?" Imran said.

The girls ignored him.

Through the tinted windows, Yacub watched the labor camp fall away behind him and the desert city draw near.

18

Michael had never lived in Toronto; for him the city remained a patchwork of locations connected by taxi rides. He never really knew where he was, occupying, as he did, hotel rooms, office buildings, and conference centers or, if he was lucky, following Marina down the street. He'd never stayed in a residential area before, so Marina's neighborhood was a revelation to him, with its streetcar stops and groovy bakeries, Whole Foods supermarket and old-timey hardware store.

Marina started every day with a long walk. "I got into the habit after Stewart died," she said. "A way to stave off"—she paused—"everything." The morning after Michael arrived, he accompanied her. They walked through streets lined with houses every bit as big, as renovated, and as manicured as Marina's, before emerging on the top lip of a hill that ran down into a ravine. The park below was full of dog walkers and runners laden with water bottles and pedometers and iPods, dressed in their bright, stretchy, waterproof, sweat-wicking clothing; Marina and Michael were soon among them, Marina in black with her black hair, Michael in an awkward getup, his work shirt, a suit jacket, plus the jeans he had bought in New York. The Toronto spring was two months behind that of London, with crocuses and daffodils only just emerging, the hillsides brown and snow-flattened, a few trees showing tentative blossom.

After their first morning out, she took him to buy some running shoes and a fleece, so he had something to wear other than his office clothes, and by their second day together, Monday, they were already into a routine: coffee, then the walk, followed by a big breakfast, after which they'd both retreat to their rooms to work, before emerging in the late afternoon ready for drinks. Michael liaised with New York and London, but without physical access to his office there wasn't a lot he could do; remote access to the company's servers had been judged too big a security risk after 9/11. He thought vaguely about heading back to New York for the week but didn't act on that notion, and no one at the company suggested it. He spent a bit of time every day talking to his assistant in London about the likelihood of getting on a flight. He said he was ready and willing to go to the airport and wait if she thought that would help.

He wasn't worried about Harriet and Jack; he knew they could cope without him. He and Harriet had played telephone tag, hobbled by the time difference and Harriet's long hours at work. They emailed—"How are you?" "We are fine. Are you okay?" "Everything fine." "Glad you're in Toronto, not New York." He'd told Harriet he was staying with Marina and she'd replied, "That's good. Glad you are safe." Michael and Jack texted each other most days— "What's up?" "Nothing—not even the planes." "Haha meh." "Love you." "Sick."

He was happy staying with Marina. And she claimed

she was happy to have him there. She wasn't working much these days. The store was doing well, she said, and she had a couple of good people running it. After Stewart died, there'd been money: various insurance payouts and death benefits. As well as that, his pension. It had seemed profoundly wrong to Marina, to find herself with money in lieu of her husband. But she hadn't turned it down, nor had she given the money away. It had, in fact, made life easier.

The news came on Tuesday that the airspace shutdown had been lifted and the first flights from London would depart that evening. On Wednesday, Michael's assistant managed to buy him the first available seat on a plane; it would leave on the weekend, Saturday night, getting him back to London Sunday morning.

Michael and Marina met for cocktails in her living room at five o'clock, as had become their habit. Earlier in the afternoon, she'd told him she was going to get dressed up. "Put on your dress pants," she said. He took a shower, combed his hair, ironed his shirt. "Pants," he thought, a word that would make Jack laugh. Michael had become accustomed to "trousers"; in England "pants" meant underwear, so the idea of "dress pants" was even more surreal.

Marina was wearing a beaded dark-gray shift dress and heels.

"This feels like a date," he said.

Marina's golden complexion became slightly rosy. "I know," she said. "Weird. But nice."

In the kitchen—which Michael had decided was in fact the Platonic ideal of a kitchen, the perfect kitchen in every way—he made gin and tonic for them both, ice and lemon, too much gin, not enough tonic, the way they liked it. In the living room they sat on the enormous long sofas and discussed where they were going to eat. Later, they took a streetcar along St. Clair and walked all the way down Spadina to have Vietnamese food at Pho Hung, Marina's favorite. She wrote their meal requests on the little pad of order forms the restaurant provided. They drank big cold glasses of Chinese beer and Marina poured chili sauce over everything, and the window they were sitting beside steamed up. After they finished, Marina suggested they walk a bit before getting a taxi, and Michael was surprised to find that when they walked down the side street behind the restaurant, they were in Kensington Market, a part of the city he hadn't visited in years. The street smelled of rotting vegetables and somewhere someone was smoking a joint. Michael felt full of nostalgia for his old self, his Canadian self, and the life he might have led had he not left his native country.

"I'd make a good Canadian."

"Once a Canadian, always a Canadian," Marina replied.

"Oh, I know that," he said, "but I mean, if I hadn't gone away." He paused. He wasn't really sure what he was trying to say. "It's strange having an English child."

Marina looked at him sideways.

"I mean, I was a Canadian boy. How is it that I have an English child?"

"Well," Marina said slowly, "my Iranian parents had me and my brothers, their Canadian children. It isn't that odd, Michael, in the scheme of things. People emigrate."

"I know, I know," said Michael, "but sometimes I dream of my Canadian life. Sometimes I worry I missed out. Canada feels— Well, you know what it feels like. Not like England."

"But you live in London—you can go to Venice for the weekend."

Michael nodded. "But what if the planes never flew again? What if crossing the Atlantic suddenly became much more difficult? What if choosing London really did mean choosing it, once and for all?"

"I'd miss you," said Marina.

"Sometimes I feel like I've led half a life in London, always the expat, never the patriot."

"Ha," said Marina. "You'd never be a patriot."

"London's problems are never really my problems, are they?"

"Toronto's stupid problems aren't my problems either," said Marina.

"I'm annoying you," he said.

"Yes, you are," she replied, smiling.

She hailed a taxi and got in. When Michael followed her, he sat down too quickly and trapped her coat so that instead of sliding across to the other window, clearing space on the seat between them, Marina was sitting right next to him. Her leg touched his. She gave the driver their destination. Michael put his arm around her shoulder. She exhaled and leaned back against him. Then she turned her face toward his, he brushed her hair away from her face, and she kissed him. He kissed her. And she kissed him again.

19

Harriet sat outside Mallory Flynn's office, waiting to go in. It was Friday morning, seven thirty, the only time Mallory could fit her in. Harriet had expected a wood-paneled, boardroom-style office, with portraits of former controllers watching from above. But instead, Mallory's office was a glass-walled box in a row of glass-walled boxes, adjacent to a vast open space that housed rows of desks and computers and, even at this time of morning, a great horde of people tapping away at their keyboards.

Mallory opened her door and said, "Harriet." She smiled and held out both her hands. They embraced quickly, and Harriet felt a soft flurry of head movements from the surrounding news desks. Mallory ushered her into her office—small, crammed with books and papers and half a dozen screens, all of which were turned on, each to a different news broadcast, a babel of newsreaders and reporters all talking at the same time. Mallory picked up a remote and pressed mute. The monitors fell silent.

"Ooh," said Harriet, "I want one of those."

"IT wizards," she said.

"You look great, Mallory," and it was true. Well-cut black suit, obedient blond hair, simple gold necklace, gold rings, gold bracelets.

"Makeup. It's all down to very expensive makeup. That stuff can make a corpse look good."

They sat down, Mallory behind her desk, Harriet wedged between the screens. "Thanks for your time."

"How are you? How's Jack, how's Michael?"

"They're good," said Harriet, "they're fine." She felt the pressure of time, the minutes ticking by on the large old-fashioned alarm clock on Mallory's desk, its round face topped with two fat bells and a clanger. "And Peter?"

Mallory had Peter when she was in her early twenties. She'd been a single parent; Peter was grown now, near the end of his medical training. "He'll finish university one day, I imagine."

"He's my friend on Facebook," Harriet said.

"You're kidding."

"He works very hard . . ."

"But he knows how to have a good time." Mallory sighed. She looked at Harriet. "What can I do for you?"

"I'm ready for a change."

"What do you mean?"

"Well," Harriet said, "radio was good for me while Jack was young, but I want to get back into television news."

Mallory raised her eyebrows. "You do?"

"I do. And I'm hoping you'll, well— I might as well just say it. Shit. Sorry. I'm hoping you'll take a look at the work I've been doing lately—it's not much—but still— I'm hoping that you'll think of me." Harriet laughed at herself, exhausted. "You know. With the election coming up—you must need people. On the ground. In the constituencies. That kind of thing?"

Mallory sat back in her chair. "The election," she said.

"Stick me out in a constituency where nothing ever happens—just in case something interesting comes along?"

"We do our election planning a long way in advance," Mallory said.

Harriet smiled hopefully.

"I'll see what I can do."

Work remained busy, if less exciting. Colleagues who'd been stranded abroad had begun to reappear. The story itself, the ash cloud and the airspace shutdown, was finished. Richmond had its old low-sky, noisy self back once again.

Friday evening, when she got home, before she did anything else, Harriet rang Michael. All week they'd been trying to connect. Six o'clock in London: one o'clock—lunchtime—in Toronto. Surely he'd be able to talk.

"Harriet?" He cleared his throat.

"Hello! My long-lost husband!"

"Won't be long now," he said. "Home Sunday."

"I know."

Michael cleared his throat again. She could hear rustling as he moved.

"Are you in bed?" she asked.

"Yeah," he said, "having a nap. I think this week of

enforced leisure has been good for me. Lots of naps. Not even power naps. Just reading a book and falling asleep."

Harriet tried to picture Michael, napping, reading. "Sounds great."

"How about you? How's Jack?"

"Jack's fine. He's had to fend for himself all week. But he's fine."

"Can I talk to him?"

"He's—he's—" Jack wasn't there. She wasn't sure where he was. "He's out with his friends."

"Oh, okay."

All the things Harriet wanted to say to her husband crashed into each other. She was missing him. She'd been too busy to dwell on that fact, but now that work was easing up, she felt his prolonged absence acutely. Mallory had put her in touch with one of the producers working on the election coverage; it looked like she was going to get the opportunity she was after.

"I saw Mallory—" she began.

"Well, I guess I'd better get up," Michael was saying at the same time. "I promised Marina I'd cook dinner tonight. I need to go get a few things."

"Oh," said Harriet. "Okay. What's the weather like there?"

"Warm. Nice. Spring is arriving."

"I'll let you go, then."

"Okay," Michael said. "Bye."

20

Jack met Frank outside the Co-op. The plan was for everyone to meet up on the high street and walk over to David McDonald's house, getting high along the way. Jack had given Ruby more cash earlier that day, to buy more weed for the party. Getting ready earlier, Jack had dressed carefully. He didn't have a lot of good clothes. He'd buy something he liked, and it would be too small for him about half an hour later. But tonight, he looked okay. Frank, on the other hand, grew at a more normal pace, and his mum liked to take him shopping. He was developing a sharp look, a kind of 1950s thing almost—narrow trousers, fitted coats, hats.

It took the others a lot of messaging and a fair amount of time to show up. First Dore, then Abdul, and finally Louise with a carrier bag full of beer—the boys handed over their cash to help pay her back for it. Now they were waiting for their entry pass, Ruby. They couldn't go to the party without Ruby. Everyone was nervous, a bit shifty: David McDonald and his friends were sixth-formers, seventeen or eighteen. Jack worried: would he and his own friends get in? Once they got in, what would they do? He'd never been to a sixth-formers' party; it felt impossibly grown-up and serious.

Still, they waited for Ruby. And waited.

"Ring her, man," said Frank.

"You ring her," said Dore.

"I don't have her number," said Frank, though everyone knew he did.

"I'll call her," said Jack, and he took his phone out of his pocket.

A car pulled up beside them. Ruby rolled down the window of the passenger seat. "Hi, everybody!" she said.

There was an older guy in the driver's seat. Ruby's brother, Jack thought, the drug dealer.

Ruby beckoned to Jack, who walked over to the car. She handed him a small, clear plastic bag.

"Oi," said the older guy. "There's a little something extra for you in there. A special treat."

"Oh," said Jack, his voice cracking as though he was stifling a shriek, "thanks."

"I'll meet you there," said Ruby.

"But—" Jack started.

"Come on, Louise," Ruby shouted, "get in the back. We'll see you guys there!"

Louise climbed into the backseat of the car, with the beer.

The boys stood on the pavement and watched Ruby and Louise drive away. Jack looked down at the bag in his hand. Tucked beneath the draw was a small silver foil packet. He shoved the bag in his pocket.

Half an hour later, they sloped up David McDonald's street. It was one of those suburban London streets that stretch on for what looks like miles without a break—a thousand houses in a single terrace, packed in tight. No front gardens, and no trees either, the road jammed with parked cars, tail to nose, no room to maneuver. They trudged along, hands in their pockets, hoods up. They could hear music in the distance.

As they got closer, other kids started to appear, heading in the same direction. Jack spotted Roman Nevsky and Lucy Cambridge. "Sixth-formers," he muttered.

"What?" said Frank.

"I saw some sixth-formers up ahead."

Frank didn't reply. A feeling of doom had descended on the boys from the moment Louise got into the car with Ruby, and that feeling grew stronger the closer they got to David McDonald's house.

The ground floor of the house was lit up, curtains open, the front door and most windows wide open too, throwing bright light onto the street. Music surged. There was a short queue to get in the front door. There was no sign of Ruby, no sign of Louise.

They waited their turn, Frank followed by Abdul followed by Dore followed by Jack. They adjusted their trousers and their jackets. Frank fiddled with his hair. The music was too loud for talking. They moved toward the door slowly. When Frank got to the top of the queue, the others crowded around him. A very short middle-aged man, possibly a man of restricted growth, Jack thought, was acting as bouncer.

"How old are you boys?" he asked. He sounded Scottish.

Frank said sixteen. Abdul said seventeen. Dore said fifteen.

Jack said eighteen.

Everyone turned to look at Jack.

"You," said the man, pointing at Jack, "you can come in. The rest of you—go home to your mothers."

Despite the man's stature, Jack could see there was no point in arguing on behalf of his friends. Frank gave him a kick from behind, and he headed into the house.

Inside, the music made the windows and floor vibrate. Jack inched his way along the entrance corridor and was funneled by the crowd up the stairs and into a room that had been emptied of furniture, apart from a DJ and his table in one corner. Up here no lights were on, but the room was a sulfury yellow, lit by the streetlights outside. Jack saw, to his mortification, that people were dancing, including, near where he was standing, Ruby and David McDonald. He turned to leave—the idea of dancing made him feel nauseated—when Ruby grabbed his arm.

"Jack! Let's do it!"

"What?" Then he remembered. He pulled the bag of draw from his pocket and held it up for her approval. She grabbed it.

"Can't smoke in here, man," said David. "My dad." He pointed toward the floor, to where his father was manning the front door below.

Ruby opened the bag and pulled out the silver packet, then handed the bag back to Jack. "Look what we've got," she said, her voice singsong and gleeful. She unwrapped the foil and revealed a small strip of paper with three tiny tablets adhering to it. She held it up for Jack and David to see. The tablets were red, each stamped with the face of a devil.

"Cool," said David.

Jack felt more nauseated. "I don't know, I—"

"More for us, then," David said. "Open up, Ruby."

Ruby tipped back her head and stuck out her tongue.

"Have fun," Jack said, and he backed out of the room, stuffing the bag of weed back into his pocket. He made his way down to the kitchen; the food was all gone, as though a pack of wolves had descended. He didn't recognize anyone. Dancing, snogging, and shouting over the music turned out to be the main things people did at sixth-formers' parties. He wandered from room to room. No sign of Louise and the beer.

How soon, he wondered, is too soon to leave?

He pulled up his hood, zipped up his coat, said thank you and good-bye to David McDonald's dad, and set off back down the street, past house after house, car after car, house after house, car after car, all the way home.

The next morning, Jack slept in, and when he got up he went straight onto his games console. He ignored his phone, not wanting to have to lie to Frank and Abdul about what a great time he had had at the party. It wasn't until after he'd had some lunch, taken a shower, got dressed, and turned on his laptop that he heard the news: David McDonald had died.

21

Imran's driver dropped Yacub off at the labor camp early the following morning. As soon as he walked into the courtyard, he knew something had changed. The food supplies donated by Imran's girls had been moved, locked away safely, he hoped, but that wasn't it. Half the doors to the rooms on his side of the block hung open. Yacub moved from door to door—the rooms were empty. The men were gone. On the second floor, the same. The last door on the second floor was closed. Yacub knocked. He heard someone stirring. He banged hard with his fist.

"Mahmoud," he shouted, "wake up."

"Okay okay okay," Mahmoud mumbled. He opened the door. Mahmoud had plans to learn to surf once he'd made his fortune. He was going to California, to ride the big wave. At least, that's what he told everybody. Yacub liked Mahmoud, he was open and friendly; sometimes he reminded him of Farhan.

"Where is everyone?"

Mahmoud rubbed his eyes and looked at Yacub. "What are you doing here? You have papers."

"I have papers—yes, of course I have papers. Where is everyone?"

"Oh man oh man oh man," said Mahmoud, shaking his head. "Bad luck bad luck bad luck, Yacub."

"What?" said Yacub. "What bad luck?"

"You, my brother. You." Mahmoud shuffled back over to his bunk and sat down. "You see, I don't have papers. I came here under a false name. Because of that business in Karachi. Stupid. It wouldn't have made any difference anyway. So I don't have papers."

"Stop talking about papers! What happened?"

"Pakistani airlift, my man. Ministry of Labour. One hundred and fifteen of them. The coaches arrived yesterday afternoon, took everyone with papers to a plane. Where were you?"

"I went with Imran and the girls."

"Ooh, what was that like?" Mahmoud's look went from mournful to lascivious. "Maybe not such bad luck after all?"

Yacub could not reply.

"Okay, I'm sorry. Listen, if you go to the council with your papers, I'm sure . . ."

But Yacub wasn't listening. He walked along the landing to the stairs. He went down to the big kitchen. A group of Indians he knew were sorting through the food supplies and cooking. "What are you doing here?" they asked. "You have papers."

"Don't ask," he replied. He slumped against the kitchen wall. His friend Ravi helped him up and over to a seat. He ate a bowl of rice and dal, but he couldn't taste it. Last night with Imran he'd eaten chicken for the first time in five months, he'd eaten chicken and thought he was the luckiest man in Dubai, while one hundred and fifteen of his Pakistani colleagues were being airlifted home without him.

The limo driver had dropped the girls off at the hotel, before delivering Yacub and Imran to Imran's surprisingly modest flat. They sat outside on plastic chairs around a plastic table and the bug zapper buzzed violently overhead every few minutes. Imran drank whiskey and talked. "If you worked for me you'd make enough money in a month to leave this place."

Yacub sipped his lemonade and nodded politely. The night air was dry and warm and the city glowed behind them.

"I am doing so well now, I don't need the construction business," Imran continued. "I work for myself. I could go back to Karachi, but what would be the point of that? There's no money for people like you and me in Pakistan." He put his arm around Yacub's shoulder. Yacub could smell the alcohol on his breath. "There's no way to get ahead."

Yacub felt bemused that Imran would speak so freely, as if the two men had something in common beyond their Pashtun heritage. If Imran wanted to pretend that they were friends for the evening, equals even, and that Yacub was not a former worker left to suffer in the dust of the abandoned labor camp, that was fine with him.

"But I'll bet you a thousand dirhams that after a month of working here, you won't want to leave. That's not a job offer, mind you," he said. "Don't get any ideas."

———

Yacub rinsed his bowl and placed it on the big metal drainer. He went to his room—his roommates were well and truly gone. He packed his few possessions into a plastic bag. Yacub set off, walking.

22

I was up and dressed and had made the house respect-
able. My son was upstairs asleep. It was eight o'clock on
Sunday morning, and I was listening to the news on the
radio in the kitchen when I heard my husband come
through the front door.

> I walked through the door and into the house.
> I had no idea what to say to my wife.

We'd been married for fourteen years.

> We'd got married the month before Jack was born;
> we moved into this house two months before that.
> My wife kept her secrets, but they were old
> secrets now. What was I going to say to her?

I called out, "Is that you?"

> "It's me," I replied. I put down my suitcase.
> I took off my coat and hung it up. I stood
> for another moment in the doorway.

"I'm in here," I said.

I went through to the kitchen. I was wearing the
new clothes that Marina had helped me buy.
Dark gray trousers, a cashmere pullover, a pair
of shoes. I'd had a haircut. I'd lost a bit of weight.
I'd brushed my teeth on the plane. I smiled at
my wife.

"Oh," I said, "you look different." I put one hand on the
counter to steady myself. "You look . . ." I stopped
talking.

I could see that she knew. "Yeah," I said,
and I nodded. "Yes."

I took a step toward him. I hadn't trusted anyone in my
life as much as I trusted Michael. It couldn't be true. But
it was true. I could see it on his face. My heart stopped
and started again, as though it was freezing. Tiny shards
of ice pierced my skin as I moved through a vast cloud of
ice toward him—my hair snapping, my face cracking,
my hands and feet becoming brittle and sharp. I felt
myself shatter. As I moved toward him I felt a great wide
surge of pain.

I watched Harriet and felt nothing. In my mind's
eye I saw Marina's hair as it fell against my face,
as she leaned low to push her body against mine.
I kept hearing that Prince song, "Purple Rain."
It took all my concentration to prevent myself

from singing. But then as I moved toward Harriet, I was overwhelmed by a terrible vertigo, as though if I looked down I'd see the earth was no longer beneath my feet. I had stepped through the front door of our house and into a gaping void, a hole, an empty sky, and I was falling out of my marriage. I was falling out of my life.

23

Upstairs, Jack was not in fact asleep but wide awake, had been for hours. Information was flooding in through his networks, and he had no idea how to tell which bits were true and which were not. David McDonald had died in Ruby's arms. David McDonald had died in the street. Six people—no, ten people—no, two people—were in intensive care, Ruby among them. Half the kids at the party had been arrested and charged with drug offenses. No one had been arrested. David McDonald had taken smack, he'd taken K, he drank a whole bottle of vodka and choked on his own vomit. He'd jumped off the roof of his house because he thought he could fly. He'd taken a little red pill with a devil's face on it that someone at the party had given him.

Jack heard his dad come through the front door, but he stayed in his room for a moment longer. He needed to figure out what to do. Ten kids had been arrested for drug offenses. Five kids. Twenty. The others were busy turning each other in. The police had a big list of kids they were picking up from their houses and taking in for questioning. David McDonald was dead. Ruby was not responding to his texts and he was too afraid of being—what, he wasn't sure: implicated?—to contact anyone else he knew had been at the party.

He closed his laptop, pulled himself together. Best to pretend nothing had happened. He'd go downstairs and say hello to his long-lost father.

Jack entered the kitchen in time to see his mother slap his father across the face.

Emily rode her bicycle up the sleepy, tree-lined street on Sunday morning. It was a picture-book southwest London suburban street with big, white, substantial houses, both terraced and detached, with front gardens and footpaths and artfully overgrown hedges, wisteria coming into flower. There was a preponderance of hybrid and electric cars parked along the street. Emily thought the whole neighborhood smelled better than where she lived, as though every room had its own subtly scented candle, every kitchen its own cappuccino machine. She spotted the house number and cycled past slowly. She paused at the end of the row of houses before turning around to cycle back.

Her skills as a researcher had come into their own as Emily parsed the posts and pages of Crazeeharree. It hadn't taken long: Crazeeharree wasn't particularly adept at hiding her identity. She was Facebook friends with a handful of Emily's friends. In fact, Crazeeharree had only one friend who wasn't also a friend of Emily's—Harriet Smith. Emily had sat back in her chair and looked at the screen. "There you are," she said. "Gotcha." Harriet Smith. She clicked. Telephone number. Place of work. Home address. She even knew Harriet's voice—her dad had had the radio tuned to that station permanently. The thought of her father and his radio had made Emily's pulse dip and she'd slumped farther into her seat.

"How am I supposed to keep going without you?" she'd said out loud. "I was looking forward to being annoyed by having to take care of you when you were old."

She cycled slowly back up the street, toward the house. The front door opened, and a woman she knew straightaway was Harriet walked out. The woman moved swiftly into the road without looking in either direction, straight over to her car. She did not look happy; she was clutching her handbag across her chest as though it was a shield. Her face was red, as though she was angry, as though she'd been crying. Emily held back, out of mirror range, she hoped, one foot on the ground for balance. Harriet started the car, pulled out, and drove away quickly.

Emily stood rigid, one foot on the ground, the other on a pedal. It was her. Emily knew it.

25

Marriage is such a fragile thing, Harriet thought. What is it? Two wedding bands and an engagement ring. A set of vows, made in front of whomever you want, wherever you want. After that, an accumulation of years. An accumulation of experiences, disappointments, and ambitions, failed and achieved. A house or flat, a bed. Sex. Children, if you're so inclined, if you're lucky. Christmas and New Year's and a few other holidays. But mostly just years. Years and years. And stuff and things.

What will happen if this marriage breaks down? What have we got to show for it, besides our stuff and our things?

After Harriet slapped Michael and saw Jack standing there in the door of the kitchen, she put on her coat, picked up her bag, and walked out of the house. She got in her car, drove across the river, and strode out along the Thames riverpath.

Tough on women, good for men, isn't that what the sociologists say about marriage? What to do, what to do? What to say? Michael had made her happy. Michael showed up when Harriet had given up on the idea of love: she was too old, too cynical, too busy for all that. She was twenty-eight. The idea of being twenty-eight almost made her smile: young, but not so young, really. She was doing well at work then, with her own little flat, her own little car, her own friends. She'd got over it, the thing that had happened, the thing that made her feel different from other people. She'd cut herself off from her own family, but she'd overcome that as well. She was fine.

Then Michael came along. They'd been together less than a year when she got pregnant. He was so sure of everything, he calculated the risk involved and made the necessary arrangements. He proposed to her and gave her a big, fat diamond engagement ring. She was shocked by how much she loved that ring. She was shocked by how happy that ring made her feel. A few swift months, fourteen years ago: they bought their house, got married, and Jack was born—bang bang bang. And ever since then they'd been . . . accumulating.

And now he'd trashed everything. It was as though he'd opened the door of the house and thrown all their possessions into the street. It had never occurred to her that Michael might be unfaithful. It had never occurred to her that he was anything less than completely trustworthy.

Life was split open. Harriet's past pushed through the crack. There were things that she regretted. Now was the time to act.

She spotted a bench farther up the path. When she reached it, she sat down and took a long look at the Thames. The tide was coming in high and the river flowed past Harriet in the wrong direction, heading inland instead of out to sea. She got out her phone and opened up Facebook to Emily's page. She couldn't contact her—not yet. She wasn't ready. But there was someone else she could try.

She did a quick search and found him: George Sigo. Most of his information was private, for friends only. She was sure it was him, though; like many people their age, he used an old photo of himself in his profile. The photo was from around the time Harriet knew him, maybe even a bit before. A young George Sigo, 1986. The year Emily was born. Harriet wrote a brief message and pressed her finger lightly on the touchscreen. Easy.

26

On Monday morning, Jack was up and dressed and ready for school early. His parents were up as well, getting ready for work. They bumped around each other in the kitchen in a way that Jack thought was oddly normal, despite what had happened the day before. Jack's mum had hit his dad. What the fuck? His dad seemed okay, but no one had ever hit anyone in Jack's house. And then, after Jack's mum hit his dad, she went out and stayed out all day. His dad spent the afternoon doing laundry and cooking. When his mum came in, she said she wasn't feeling great and went upstairs to lie down. Jack and his dad ate dinner together and tried to converse, but Jack's head was too full of unmentionables—his parents' row, of course, which he did not want to talk about, but mainly David McDonald, and Ruby—he still hadn't heard from Ruby. David McDonald was dead, and Jack did not want to have to tell his father he'd been at the party. Luckily for Jack, he wasn't asking questions.

There was the problem of the bag of weed. He'd given the tablets to Ruby and had left the party with the bag of weed. Jack had to get rid of it. If the rumors were correct and the police were questioning everyone who had been to the party . . . his name might well be on some list somewhere. And the police might arrive, and they might search the house, and then what would happen? Jack pictured police officers rooting around his bedroom. If they found the drugs, maybe he'd be accused of dealing. They'd do their forensic thing on it and discover there'd been other drugs in the bag, and that maybe David McDonald had taken those missing drugs, and that maybe that was what had killed him. And that Jack was, in fact, responsible for his death.

He had to get rid of that bag. He'd take it to school. He'd find Ruby—where was Ruby?—and ask her to give it back to her brother. He wasn't expecting his money back or anything like that, he knew Ruby's brother wouldn't offer sale or return, refunds within twenty-eight days, money-back guarantee. But it seemed like the most logical thing to do—get the drugs back to the drug dealer, where they belonged.

So Jack packed his lunch and packed his school bag and got together his PE kit for football training after school. His mother offered him an apple, and he agreed to take it because he knew it would make her happy. At the last minute, he ran back upstairs and pulled the little plastic bag out from where he'd hidden it inside his old piggybank—"Acorn-fed Iberian *jamón*!" his father used to say whenever Jack got out the piggybank—and thinking about this now, the innocence of it, his parents and their middle-class ways, made Jack want to cry.

He ran back down the stairs and, once again, his parents were having some kind of a face-off in the kitchen, though this time no one was hitting anyone else. He said good-bye to them both without breaking his stride, though he saw a sadness, a despair on both their faces that he'd never seen before. Out the front door, into the April sunshine, and down the street.

Jack was alarmed to see two uniformed officers in the parking lot of the school. He waved at a few of his friends but kept his head down and went straight into the library, where he knew he'd be left to his own devices. In the corridor there were new notices stating "COUNSELLING AVAILABLE." He passed a huddle of sixth-formers, several of whom were crying. Most of the staff was back at work by now, but the school had a hush to it, as unusual as the absence of planes had been the previous Monday.

In his form group, the teacher, Mr. Rushdie (not a popular member of staff; otherwise known as Fatwa, though Jack had no idea why) stood up, cleared his throat, looked uncomfortable, and said, "I'm sure you've heard the very sad news regarding David McDonald. I don't have any other information to give you; there'll be an assembly later this week. The police are here in case anyone has any information they'd like to pass on; you can talk to me or talk to them directly. Classes will proceed as normal. Have a good day."

Fatwa had never told them to have a good day before. That in itself was disconcerting.

At first break Jack rushed over to the far side of the playing field, near the trees, where Ruby usually hung out with their friends. There was no sign of her. A group of kids was standing in a tight circle. Jack nudged Frank to one side so he could get in and see what was happening. Louise was standing in the middle and she was crying.

"Fuck, that's bad," Abdul was saying, shaking his head. "Really bad."

"Why'd you come in today?" Frank asked her. "Did your mum make you?"

Louise nodded, but she couldn't speak. The other girls had their arms around her.

"We were there," Frank said. "God."

Jack looked around sharply, trying to see where those police officers were. "Where's Ruby?" he asked Louise.

Everyone looked at him as though he was an idiot.

"She's in hospital—didn't you know?" one of the other girls said.

"Hospital?" said Jack.

"Don't you know anything?" Abdul asked. "Weren't you there?"

Frank stepped away from the group, motioning to Jack to follow him, as if he didn't want the others—Jack guessed Louise—to hear what he had to say. "Look, man, they took a bunch of stuff," said Frank. "Ruby, David McDonald, I don't know who else—five of them. They all got really sick. David had something wrong with his heart that they didn't know about. It stopped. He died. The other four, they're in hospital. But they're not dead. And they're not going to die."

"Where'd they get the drugs from?"

Frank shook his head. "No idea." He lowered his voice further. "Ruby, don't you think?"

"Shit."

"Full police investigation," Frank said, knowledgeably. "They've got the names of everyone who was at the party."

"Why are you going around saying you were there, then?" Jack asked.

"There's a difference between actually being on the list and saying you're on the list."

Jack snorted.

"But you're on the list, Jack, I'm sure."

Frank returned to the huddle around Louise. Jack walked across the tarmac toward the school, not completely sure where he was going. What was he going to do with the bag of weed? He couldn't just throw it away—what if the rumor that there were surveillance cameras hidden all over the school was true? Jesus. What was he fucking going to do with the motherfucking drugs he was carrying in his bag?

27

Two days after he replied to her message, Harriet arranged to meet George Sigo in a pub in Brixton. She hadn't been to Brixton since the 1980s. It was changed and yet unchanged, like most of London, a little more gentrified, a little smarter around the edges. There are bits of London that feel newer now than they did in the past, as if getting richer had made the city younger as well, but less authentic too, more plastic, like a rich old woman with a brightly sliced and pulled-taut face. Brixton had that feeling in parts, though the dense crowd still rushed from the tube station up to the bus stops along the pavement. Harriet walked down Electric Avenue, unsure whether she was hearing music for real or hearing music from her memory.

The pub was just the same, the same old men playing dominoes out back, the same Eddy Grant record playing. It was four o'clock in the afternoon, so the place was nearly empty. Harriet sat at a table with a view of the door, waiting for George Sigo.

He looked the same, if a little craggier, as though time had roughed him up instead of aging him. He still had his black Irish good looks, though his short dark hair was flecked with gray. She hadn't known him well, really. And then he'd gone to prison, something to do with his

Republican politics; she'd taken care to stay well clear of anything to do with that. She'd wanted nothing more to do with him, in fact. She disappeared from her old life, changing her name when she married Michael. She was untraceable, she thought. And here she was, at her own instigation, revealed.

"George," she said.

He stood in front of her and did not look friendly.

"Take a seat," she said. "Let me get you a drink."

He nodded, said, "I'll have a pint of ale," and took off his jacket, hanging it over the back of a chair, straightening the shoulders before sitting down carefully. Harriet squeezed by him to get to the bar. As she ordered their drinks she could tell he was watching, staring at her, measuring. He stood up and came toward her. The barman was pulling the pint of ale; he'd poured Harriet's ginger beer already. Harriet took a few steps along the bar, closer to the barman.

"I looked for you, Harriet," George said.

"Why don't you sit down?"

George nodded, but he didn't move as Harriet got out her purse. She noticed the barman was watching them both closely. She picked up the drinks and walked back to the table.

She sat. George followed but remained standing. He towered over her. He was dressed in fitted black trousers, a slim white shirt, the jacket he'd hung so carefully on the chair, and a skinny black tie, as though it was still the 1980s. "I looked for you when I got out," he said, "for the better part of a decade."

"I went my own way. I thought it was for the best."

"Why have you contacted me now?"

"Why don't you sit down?"

He didn't.

"Well," Harriet said, "I thought I should tell you." She stopped. "A lot of time has gone by."

"Too much time," said George.

"What have you been doing all these years?" Harriet asked. How could she have been so rash? Why had getting in touch with him seemed like a good idea? A reaction to what had happened with Michael? Stupid. Childish. She still hadn't talked to Michael since he arrived home; she hadn't told him she was meeting George Sigo.

"What are you doing here, Harriet?" He moved closer to where she was sitting, took hold of her shoulder, and squeezed it hard. "Tell me," he said, "where she is."

Harriet winced and attempted to pull away.

"Hey, George." The barman had come out from behind the bar. He was standing behind George, who turned to look at him, allowing Harriet to free herself from George's grip. She moved around the table to a stool on the other side. "How've you been lately?" the barman continued.

George's tone softened slightly. "I'm fine, Craig," he said. "Doing fine."

"Are you taking your meds?" Craig asked. "You know you're not allowed in here unless you're taking your meds and keeping your appointments." Craig looked at Harriet and smiled, as though this was common knowledge. "He forgets to take them sometimes. Then he ends up back on the ward and banned from here. And no one's happy."

"Oh for fuck's sake, Craig. You're not my daddy." George reached for his jacket. He pulled a hospital card out of the inside pocket and handed it to the barman.

Craig looked at it. He looked at Harriet, nodding, as though they were complicit in some way. "It's such a shame you need to leave. But you're late, aren't you? For that thing."

"Late," said Harriet. She understood. She stood up and put on her coat. "I am late. Thanks for reminding me."

"No problem," the barman said. "Another time, eh, George?"

Harriet, flustered, dropped her bag. She stooped to pick it up, and as she stood, George grabbed her once again. The young barman took hold of George's arm.

"George," Craig said, his voice full of warning.

George pushed his face close to Harriet's. She could smell his breath: yeasty, like rising bread.

"What's her name?" he asked.

"Who?" said Harriet, but she knew who he meant.

"She'll be twenty-four now. What's her name?"

The barman gave George's arm a yank, which succeeded in throwing him off balance. He let go of Harriet.

She walked toward the door as quickly as she could. She opened it wide and sunlight flooded into the dim bar. As she crossed the threshold, she heard George Sigo speak once again. "I know *your* name now," he said. "I know where to find *you*."

28

It took Yacub the whole day to walk across Dubai from the labor camp to the hotel where Imran conducted his business. Dubai is not a pedestrian-friendly city. Even Karachi with its broken-down pavements and roads, its sandbagged and gun-turreted buildings, was easier to get around by foot. Yacub mostly walked in the dirt at the side of the highway; cars rushed by, the hot churning wind slammed against him, and the sun beat down on his bare neck. He was wearing his oldest shalwar kameez, but the thin material still felt too heavy.

The hotel was enormous, set between the road and the canal, surrounded by vast landscaped grounds and building sites. The front entrance was accessed via a long drive; this was not the way the hotel workers normally arrived. Yacub saw a lorry turn in farther along the road, so he made his way round the side of the hotel, where he found the trade entrance. The sun was setting as he slipped into the hotel behind a man pushing a shrink-wrapped pallet of goods. He walked through the unadorned service area, down its battered corridors until he found a men's room. There, he gulped water direct from the tap before washing in the sink; from his carrier bag, he retrieved his only decent pair of Western-style trousers and his only good shirt, left over from his time working in Karachi.

Once dressed, he inspected himself in the mirror over the sink. Now he looked like a lowly clerk, which was better than a lowly laborer.

Yacub grabbed his plastic bag of dirty clothes and made his way through the hotel. Last night Imran had declared that the twenty-eighth floor of this hotel belonged to him, and Yacub remembered this as he made his way from the service area into the plush, air-conditioned splendor of the hotel itself. The carpet was thick beneath his feet and the foyer was populated by giant floral displays scenting the already perfumed air. He found his way to the elevators. As he stood there, unsure of what to do next, one of the sets of doors opened and a European man in a suit got out. Yacub stepped inside. A European woman, also wearing a suit, was in the elevator already; she frowned at him. Soft music played in the background. The woman got out at the twentieth floor. The doors closed. For a moment, nothing happened. The music continued to play but the elevator didn't move. Yacub pressed the number 28.

On the twenty-eighth floor the doors opened to the sound of pulsing music. Yacub hesitated, then stepped out as the doors began to slide shut. To his left, a set of double doors were slightly ajar. Yacub stood at the threshold, pushed the door a little more open, and looked in. The large room was kitted out like a nightclub, with a bar along one wall, tables and chairs around a small dance floor where one woman danced slowly. Colored lights flashed overhead while low lamps spread minimal light through the rest of the room. A small crowd of European men stood by the bar. As he stared through the darkness, Yacub made out a seating area with plump sofas and low chairs and a number of Asian women sitting on the sofas, as well as on the high stools off to one side of the dance floor. Yacub stepped into the room and stood still as the lights flashed blue, red, and green across his white shirt.

Two of the Pakistani girls from yesterday's limo were seated on high stools near the door. "Hello, sir," one said, smiling sweetly, and Yacub could see she recognized him. He dipped his head in her direction. At that moment, Imran strode into the room.

"Okay," he said, looking at Yacub. "Take this receipt down to the service area. A porter will help you bring the order up."

Yacub took the piece of paper. He felt stunned by the colored lights and the sofas and the girls—the entire room and the world it contained.

"I know," Imran said, and paused. "You missed the airlift."

Yacub swallowed hard and looked down at the receipt he was holding.

"Go on. Get on with it."

29

The plan Michael made during the flight from Toronto was simple: say nothing.

He had no intention of leaving Harriet, he had no intention of moving to Toronto and taking up with Marina. He had no desire to explain himself. He couldn't explain himself, in fact. He had no idea why he'd done what he'd done. Nothing had changed. Nothing was going to change. He was not going to explain a thing.

While Michael was in Toronto, he watched CBC news and listened to CBC radio; he read *the Globe and Mail* and *National Post* newspapers; he bought *The Walrus* magazine. He watched *Hockey Night in Canada* with Marina. He measured his Canadian pulse, his Canadian heart rate. It beat on, as regular as ever. He wasn't sure what exactly made him Canadian, but the unexpected week in Toronto confirmed it: he was. But he lived in London; London was his life.

Marina had been upset when they said good-bye. "I wish we hadn't done this," she said.

"But it has been really, really, great."

"I know," she said. "Now I'll miss you. Before I never would have missed you."

"Our ash cloud idyll," Michael said.

"Our ash cloud paradise," Marina replied. "*Mein lieben* Dick Schwein."

He pulled her close. She sighed. Then he got into his waiting taxi.

He hadn't reckoned on the fact that Harriet would know. He walked in the door with his suitcase, looked at her, and she knew.

And Michael didn't have a fucking clue what to do about it. So he ironed his shirt and went back to work, where risk was theoretically quantifiable.

30

The atmosphere both at home and at school remained very strange. At home, Jack's dad returned to his normal long hours at work, and Jack's mum was also busy. She was much more on edge than was normal, locking windows, locking doors, spending hours on the computer in the evening. He was surprised that they hadn't asked about David McDonald; the story had been in the local paper, though the school was not named. Neither of them seemed to have heard a thing about it and Jack wasn't about to volunteer any information.

At school the atmosphere remained subdued; groups of girls still spent time huddled in the corridors crying. It felt as though everyone, from the most senior teachers to the youngest of students, had decided the right response to David McDonald's death was to behave as though he had been their closest friend in the world and they didn't know how to continue without him. Jack knew full well that to most kids in the school, himself included, David McDonald was a name and an image— tall, a bit mean-looking—nothing more. The longest and only conversation Jack had ever had with him was last Friday night with Ruby.

The police were still hanging around the school. The

rumor was that conversations between police, teachers, and the sixth form had revealed that the school had its very own rather large recreational drug economy. Jack had spent most of the past week sweating and paranoid at school during the day, sweating and worrying at night. But he'd finally found a solution to his problem.

FRANK: sUre ill take em off u
JACK: really?
FRANK: no problemo LOL
JACK: gr8
FRANK: c U by the portacabin at brk

Jack left his maths class and made his way outside. He could see Frank standing there, and it was all he could do not to run to him and throw his arms around him. He reached into the inside pocket of his backpack and pulled out the plastic bag. The weed was fairly pulverized after being stashed and stored and hidden, and one of the bag's corners was slightly torn. As Jack handed it over, a little trail of weed dust fell down the front of Frank's trousers. Frank stuffed the plastic bag deep into his backpack.

"Not every day that I get given something for nothing," Frank said.

Jack felt so relieved he was almost floating. "Think of it as all the birthday and Christmas presents I'll never give you rolled into one."

The bell rang. Frank sloped off. Jack stood where he

was, trying to remember where he was supposed to be. He watched as Frank rounded the corner of the portacabin and walked straight into the two friendly police officers, who, for the first time that week, were there with a sniffer dog.

Very bright light shining in her eyes. She was prepared for this. Over the past three weeks she'd talked herself up for it, written and rewritten, rehearsed and re-rehearsed, but she had forgotten what it actually felt like; it had been a long time since she'd been live on camera. Microphone on her lapel, earpiece in, so she could hear the producers— one here in the hall, standing next to the cameraman, the others down in London with their election-night holograms and graphics. It was two o'clock in the morning; she had planned to arrive before lunchtime. Sweating.

"Why are you so fucking late?" the producer had hissed at Harriet when she ran through the door, Jack trailing behind her.

"It's a long story." She attempted to keep her voice low, but Jack heard her anyway.

"A guy tried to kill us," he said, his voice calm.

Harriet had left London much later than she had planned and there had been numerous and increasingly irate phone calls from the producer as she drove up the motorway. Then a long deviation from her intended route as she attempted to lose George Sigo. "It's all right," Harriet said, to reassure the producer as well as Jack. "It's over now. We're here."

The producer looked at Jack. She had sharply cut black hair and heavy black-rimmed designer spectacles, and she was juggling two BlackBerrys and a laptop. She spoke to Harriet while continuing to stare at Jack. "You bring your child to a live broadcast? Very professional."

Harriet spread her hands and shrugged, hoping for a smidgeon of female solidarity. Jack had been suspended from school for a month. Despite the fact that Harriet and Michael weren't officially talking to each other, there had been hours of family conversations about what had happened at that party the night that boy had died. It was Michael's idea that Jack accompany her today. "Take him. A live election night broadcast; it will be interesting for him." She'd been pleased by the suggestion. That was before she'd spotted George Sigo sitting in a car outside their house.

"A guy actually tried to kill us," Jack said. "A psycho. He chased us in his car. Aren't you a journalist or something? There's a story here."

A technician was behind Harriet now, fiddling with the wire that ran up the back of her jacket.

"No," the producer said loudly, "we do not need Television Centre to take over this count. We are on it." She was speaking to London. She moved her own mic away from her face to speak to Harriet again. "You're lucky they dropped a box of ballots and had to do a recount. If you don't get it together we'll lose this broadcast—I've been fending them off all evening. Who are you, anyway? Why have they landed me with you?"

Harriet got her mirror out of her bag and took a look at herself.

"Last election," the woman continued, "I worked with Martha Kearney. Martha Kearney! What kind of fuckery are you involved with?"

"Local radio," Harriet said, though she wasn't entirely sure what the producer's question meant.

"Local radio. Great."

A voice in Harriet's earpiece: "The candidates are getting up on the stage."

Jack stood behind the cameraman. Harriet wanted him where she could see him, and he wanted to be where he could see her; ever since Jack had been suspended from school, he'd stuck close to his mother. The candidates lined up behind Harriet on the stage, a rumpled-looking group that included the Tory with a heavy five o'clock shadow, the LibDem in a yellow dress, the Labour candidate looking mournful, as well as two fringe candidates— a member of the Flying Nun Party in her habit and a member of the Monster Raving Loony Party dressed as Frankenstein and holding a guitar. Harriet had written a short script, she had memorized it. This was her chance. Mallory had given her this opportunity. What happened today with George— being pursued by him, shouting at him in the petrol station forecourt—she had to push it out of her mind. Jack was safe. Harriet didn't know what was going to happen to her marriage, but Michael was home and would be watching. She needed to show Michael and

Mallory and Jack as well as this bloody producer that she could do this. Concentrate.

In the monitor in her line of vision, she could see them hard at it in Television Centre.

"Over to Harriet in ten," said the voice in her earpiece.

She counted. The green light on the camera went on. The election official was droning away in the background. Very bright light shining in her eyes. The producer waved. The monitor was showing a hall full of ballot boxes, party supporters, election officials, and there, beside the stage, a middle-aged woman in a dark red jacket. Harriet. She began to speak.

"Here at Tipton Mallet—a town unaccustomed to media attention—the battle for votes has been intense. Last year's unfortunate death of the Labour incumbent, Simon Taylor, MP for twenty-five years, combined with the accusations of Conservative Party HQ interference in candidate selection, and the unexpectedly high ratings in the polls for Geraldine Coogan, the Liberal Democrat candidate, have created a firestorm of political—"

Out of the corner of her eye, she saw George Sigo. She stopped speaking. He was walking toward her. She looked back at the camera. George Sigo was heading toward her. Voice from London in her earpiece: "Come on, speak! Speak!"

The producer started waving her arms.

"A firestorm of political intrigue," she continued. "It's an open field here, David; the gloves are off."

On the monitor, the man in Television Centre smiled. "What's the atmosphere in the hall like, Harriet?"

"Tense," she said. "Trepidation."

Harriet looked at George. He looked at her.

"No one knows what's going to happen."

George Sigo charged, head down, and grabbed Harriet around the waist. He lifted her onto the stage. Then he continued to push her backward into the line of candidates. Frankenstein fell, then the Flying Nun, and another, and another.

The producer screamed.

Or was it Harriet?

PART TWO

FLYING MAN

SPRING 2012

1

I cycle behind her car down the street, veering off
at the roundabout as she turns into the supermarket.

There is almost no room for me on this shelf; there is no
secret entrance into the cargo hold.

I finish the shopping beneath the supermarket's
harsh lights and zombie-walk Muzak; the boy
at the checkout is unaccountably cheerful,
and this makes me smile.

I've been watching her for so long;
today is no different.

I am crushed into this too-small space; I have been here
for an eternity.

I push the loaded trolley across the car park,
battling to keep its wonky wheels on track as
it veers toward a row of shiny bumpers.

I ride home and climb the stairs to my flat.

Freezing hot, then burning cold.

I pop open the boot of my car and then for
some reason, I have no idea why, I look up,
into the clear blue sky.

Suddenly, I am released.

The woman who might be my mother looks up
into the sky—looks up and continues looking up.

And I see him.

And then, through the eye of my camera,
I see him.

I am free.

It takes me a long moment to figure out
what I am looking at.

A man in the sky, falling.

I am flying.

A dark mass, growing larger quickly.

I am falling through the sky.

Landing Gear

He is falling from the sky.

The earth is coming up to meet me.

I let go of the trolley but I can't move and am
dimly aware that it is getting away from me.
I am stuck in the middle of the supermarket
car park, watching as he hurtles toward me.

I nearly knock over my camera, but I steady
myself and find him again.

Almost there now, my destination.

I have no idea how long it takes—a few seconds,
an entire lifetime—but I hold my breath as the
suburbs go about their business around
me until . . .

I've arrived, at last.

He crashes into the roof of her car.

2

Filming the falling man was accidental. It was a calm, clear morning, midweek, spring. Emily had the day off; she was waiting for Harriet to come out of her house. She'd been following her for the better part of two years, on and off. As far as she could tell, Harriet was oblivious. As usual, around ten, Harriet got in her car. Emily lurked farther up the street on her bicycle; these days, Harriet never seemed to leave Richmond, and it had proved easy to follow her around by bike, helmet and cycling gear helping to obscure her identity. Emily had to be careful, since Harriet knew what she looked like from Facebook.

As usual Harriet was well dressed, makeup perfect, "camera-ready." Emily knew from watching her for so long that Harriet liked to be prepared. Her taste in clothes ran to the more expensive end of standard newsreader with a slight overreliance on dark colors. She could tell Harriet hadn't bought new clothes since losing her job two years before, after that extraordinary—what to call it?—*incident* during the election broadcast. But she looked fine now, pulled together in that not-without-a-struggle, midforties way. Thicker through the waist than she would have been twenty years before, but this was not muffin-top, bulge, or spilling-out-of-a-bra territory. Good legs.

There'd been many surprises as Emily researched Crazeeharree, not the least of which was that she lived in the same corner of London—Harriet in the posh, leafy bit, Emily in the flats near the supermarket and the roundabout and the railway sidings, ten minutes away by bike. They both worked in media—at least Harriet had, before she lost her job. They both—

Emily stopped herself. She knew nothing about Harriet. In the past two years she had vacillated, one moment sure this woman must be her mother, the next minute sure she was not. In the morning she'd wake up convinced today was the day to make contact; by the time she looked in the bathroom mirror she'd have decided that today was not the day after all. She didn't need a mother, she'd had her dad, and now she had his memory. She allowed Crazeeharree to be her friend on Facebook; in turn, she followed her around on her bike. It was a relationship, of sorts.

Harriet got in her car and Emily followed her as she drove, as usual, to the supermarket. Was it possible for one woman to go to the supermarket with any greater frequency? Not unless she worked there, Emily thought, and Harriet would have to be much more severely reduced in circumstances and outlook before she would work in a supermarket. At the roundabout, Emily veered off toward her block of flats. She locked up her bike, climbed the four floors of stairs—there was no lift, which was why she could afford the flat—and installed herself with tripod and video camera in time to see Harriet's car—red, the roof splattered with birdshit and tree droppings, as always—pull into a parking spot. Harriet went into the store, which Emily figured would allow enough time to make a cup of tea.

Emily had started filming Harriet right after she imploded on live television; she now had an enormous archive of the woman going about her business, which primarily meant going to the supermarket. Tea made, Emily sat back down at the window and double-checked her equipment. She'd had the idea of filming from the window of her flat last month: Harriet in her car in the supermarket car park, arriving and departing—anything to give the footage a bit of variety. Emily was planning one of those epic, so-boring-it's-profound documentaries about this middle-aged, unemployed, wealthy woman's life, with a big-bang surprise ending, the artifice of the documentary revealed and a true story—and the film-maker's own connection to it—told to devastating effect. Good graphics, moody music, solemn voice-over. Web campaign. She knew it was weird, but she didn't care. Filming Harriet had become part of how Emily lived.

Harriet had been inside the shop for ages, but her red car was still in the car park, so everything was fine. Warm air floated in through the open window; it was March but felt more like June. Emily drank her tea and listened to the radio. It was soothing, sitting in a patch of sun, watching people come and go in the car park, the sound of planes overhead, their regular and unceasing rhythm.

Another ten minutes passed and Harriet appeared, pushing a trolley with a remarkable amount of food in it.

There was only one kid and one husband living with her in the big house; either they ate a huge amount or the woman cooked a ton and threw it all away. Emily filmed as Harriet pushed the trolley to the car and opened the boot. But instead of loading the bags, Harriet stopped abruptly and looked up into the sky. She continued to stare upward so Emily followed her gaze with the camera.

And then, through the eye of her video camera, she saw him. A man in the sky, falling. A plane continuing to Heathrow. She was so startled she nearly knocked the camera over, but she steadied herself and found him in the sky again. And then, bang.

He crashed into the roof of Harriet's car.

Emily shouted and stood up, kicking over the tripod. She picked up the camera quickly and refocused. The falling man was lying on the roof of Harriet's car, which had crumpled around him like a metal hammock. Harriet was standing beside the car, she had let go of her trolley, and it was rolling away from her down the slight incline. The rest of the car park was still, the road next to it free of traffic, the London suburbs embraced by that familiar midmorning lull when everyone is at work or school or indoors drinking coffee. A moment of peace to mark a man's fall from the sky. He's dead, Emily thought, he's gone. He has passed from his world to this world and beyond.

Another plane flew overhead and a convoy of lorries circled the roundabout before barreling away. The falling man sat up and looked around. He climbed down off the wrecked car and Emily filmed as Harriet stepped back.

The man retrieved the errant shopping trolley and began to talk to Harriet, who got her phone out of her bag and made a call. To Emily's amazement, after a few short minutes, a mini-cab pulled up, and Harriet and the falling man put the shopping bags in the back of the taxi before climbing inside and driving away.

Once they had gone, Emily sat on the floor of her flat, staring at a bit of carpet that was beginning to fray. She'd bought the carpet in a souk in Morocco. It was a quiet market, with very few tourists and no hard sell, so for once she felt able to buy something. She'd bargained but could no longer remember what she had paid, whether it was ten pounds or a hundred, even though the price had seemed all-important at the time. The seller had told her the carpet's history, where it had been made, by whom, but she'd forgotten long since. She'd always wanted a magic carpet, and this seemed like a decent substitute.

Emily was crying a little bit and shivering. What had she just seen? Was it real? What did it mean? Could this be an elaborate ruse to smuggle illegal immigrants into the country, a scam that Harriet was involved in? No, that was ridiculous. And she had looked as shocked as Emily was to see a man falling from the sky.

Eventually, she got up, retrieved the camera, and sat down on the sofa. Rewind, play. Rewind, play. It was there, she had captured it, and it was real, she hadn't photoshopped it, it wasn't from YouTube, she'd seen it happen with her own eyes. Freeze-frame. She downloaded it to her laptop. She copied it onto an external drive as well as a memory stick and deposited these in her usual hiding places around the flat. Then she worked on the footage, breaking it down into a series of still images and video fragments.

This was not what Emily had anticipated would happen in her film of Harriet's life. Even though she was still shocked by what she had seen, she knew already that this was much better than the intervention she had planned. This would take the film in an entirely different direction. She needed to think this through.

She watched the footage yet again, still shivering. Then she posted on a Twitter account she used only occasionally: "Is it a plane? Is it a bird? Or is it a man, falling?"—followed by a single image. She didn't want to use Facebook: Harriet would know straightaway that the photo had come from her. Emily wondered if Harriet would see the tweet. She sat back in her chair; she hoped Harriet would find it. Why else post it?

3

In the days before Yacub arrived, Harriet fixed up the little room at the back of the kitchen. She wasn't sure why. She felt as though someone was coming to visit, approaching from afar, and that person was going to need a place to stay. She had a strong sense of needing to get ready, like when she found herself cleaning kitchen cupboards before she gave birth to Jack. Now she was glad the room was ready. Yacub might be dead, but even the dead need a place to lay their heads, otherwise they might wander around the house all night, wailing and moaning.

A man fell out of the sky: she could scarcely bring herself to think about it. "Am I dead?" he had asked as he climbed down off the roof of her car. "Am *I?*" she had replied. Harriet was sure that she herself was alive. The kitchen floor was still dirty—what more proof did she need? She had seen someone fall from a great height once before, and there was no denying her condition on landing. That young woman was dying, and as Harriet held her hand, her friend's life drained away. If Yacub was not dead, well, Harriet didn't believe in magic. She didn't believe in ghosts either, not really, except . . . Yacub was as cold as a dead man. In the taxi on the way home from the supermarket, he had started to shiver violently. When

Harriet took off her scarf and placed it around his shoulders, she had touched his hand; it felt like a chicken fillet, fresh out of the freezer.

There'd been a man a couple of years before—a Romanian, Harriet recalled—who'd survived a flight from Vienna to London, stashed in the plane's landing gear. He'd walked away from his journey, dazed but unscathed. But that was when the leftover ash cloud from the Icelandic volcano was still roaming around European airspace, and the plane had been flying at a low altitude. Harriet thought she could remember other stories—half read in newspapers or online—about people surviving much longer, more perilous journeys, similar to what Yacub had undertaken. In the mini-cab, teeth chattering, he'd told her his name and said he'd come from Karachi. His English was good. He wanted to know where he was and when she told him—Richmond, London, England—he'd looked disappointed. She had to admit, he might be alive. Then again, if he'd survived the journey, how could he have survived the great fall that ended it?

It made sense for the supermarket to be the place where it happened. It shimmered beside the roundabout, full of promise, the great piles of produce, the vast displays of meat, the superabundance of choice, enough cans and boxes and bottles to feed the whole of Richmond for weeks. Harriet liked to go there because, as soon as she entered through the whispering glass doors, she felt a sense of purpose that her life otherwise denied her. Jack was growing up. Michael worked. It wasn't as though she'd ever wanted to be a housewife, a stay-at-home mum, a full-time mother, terms she found equally repellent and imprecise. In the supermarket, all of it—what she had desired for her own life, what she had lost along the way—faded. She listened to the scanners beep. She filled her trolley. She felt secure, replete.

The evening of the day that Yacub fell on Harriet's car, it was just Jack and Harriet for supper, as usual, Michael working late. Jack didn't get home till after six—sports or hanging out with his friends, or both, she didn't like to ask, or rather, she did like to ask, but he didn't like her to ask, so she didn't. Today, bringing Yacub home with the bags of shopping, she was grateful he wasn't back from school yet, regardless of whether Yacub was a ghost or not. Who knew whether other people would be able to see him? When Jack came in, he dropped his school bag, kicked off his shoes, turned on the games console, and went online while Harriet cooked. She felt happy in the kitchen with Jack in the sitting room, knowing that if Yacub emerged from the little room where she'd put him, she could head him off at the pass. She made a meal that she knew Jack would like, and she didn't ask him to set the table.

Harriet had given up asking Jack to set the table a couple of years back when his response to her request was such a gush of teenage hostility that she screeched at him that if he didn't set the table *right now* she would never cook him dinner ever again. He laughed, of course. She knew that he knew the threat was meaningless and that she would be unable to act upon it no matter how hard she stamped her feet. She knew he knew that the result would be the polar opposite of the threat: she would not only continue to cook dinner for him every night, she would never ask him to set the table ever again. So she cooked, and she set the table, and peace reigned: Harriet in the kitchen, Jack on his games console, Yacub asleep in the little room off the kitchen, Michael at work.

Yacub had to be dead. Or, Harriet reasoned, she might have done what her son had long been suggesting: lost her mind.

She turned on the radio, half expecting to hear her own voice on it. If a man could fall out of the sky and survive, surely she could be in two places at the same time?

4

Yacub liked the room the woman put him in. The walls lined up with the floors. The window had two layers of glass in it and curtains. The door had a knob and a lock with a key in it. There were power outlets and shelves above a little table with a chair and a lamp, and a bed with sheets and blankets and pillows that were soft. There was a rug on the floor. Very very clean, everything clean, everything lined up straight. Tidy. New. He ran his hands back and forth over the bed, trying to convince himself it was real.

When they arrived at the house, she sat him down at the kitchen counter and wrapped a soft, tasseled blanket around his shoulders before making him a sandwich and a mug of milky tea. The kitchen was like something out of a movie. Not quite an American kitchen. But not like a kitchen he'd ever sat in before: they cooked on a fire at his father's house in the Swat Valley, he had served food from a dim old kitchen in that house in Karachi, and in Dubai hundreds of men had jostled for space in the labor camp's communal kitchen. He'd left his home and gone to work in Karachi; he'd left Karachi and gone to work in Dubai; he'd left Dubai and gone home to Pakistan where he paid Ameer to get him onto the plane that brought him here. He ached from his arduous journey. As he sat in that kitchen, he wanted to put his face down on the cool, clean, shiny counter, black with flecks of silver and gold beneath the hard surface. She saw that he was tired and so she showed him the room.

"You'll be safe in here," she said. "If you hear my family, just stay in your room. In case, well—in case you're dead. We don't want to alarm them." She smiled and closed the door. Yacub listened, but she did not lock it from the outside.

Yacub was happy to stay in the room. There had been a lot of times in his life when he was confined or restricted, though never in such conditions of luxury. He lay down under the covers—layers of blankets and duvets—and fell into a deep, dark sleep.

In his sleep, he dreamed of flying. Not hunched up on a tiny shelf beneath the plane's undercarriage, or packed into an old PIA plane with only a plastic bag for his luggage. He dreamed of flying through the soft night air above the green valley where he was born. Flying without effort, weightless and airborne, like the kites and gulls he used to watch hovering over Karachi. In Dubai he'd been amazed when Imran had shown him Google Earth on the glossy tablet an American client had given him to make good a debt. At first the sensitive touchscreen had alarmed Yacub, but only briefly. He used it to fly himself over the Arabian Sea, pausing over Karachi, then following the Indus and its tributaries up to the Swat Valley. He dropped down to a lower altitude to try to find his village, but the map had pixelated and frozen, and Imran had decided it was time to leave. But still, what he'd seen had entered Yacub's dreams; when he dreamed of flying now, he flew via satellite.

When he woke up, the house was completely quiet, as was the street outside: nighttime. He switched on the lamp and noticed a plate with another sandwich and a glass of water beside it: did they eat nothing but sandwiches in England? There was a note as well but the handwriting was of poor quality and he could not read it. He tried to imagine what it might say, but there were too many possibilities: "Enjoy the sandwich and make yourself at home." "Enjoy the sandwich but leave immediately as my husband will kill you when he finds you." "Enjoy the sandwich, there's plenty more where this came from, but I'll make you pay for it by ensuring you become our family house slave."

Yacub had worked for a wealthy family in Karachi, and he was not going back to that again. In many ways his time working in that household was worse than his time working in Dubai, even after the building company was bankrupted. Of course the worst time of all was on that frozen shelf behind the giant burning wheels beneath the plane. But he'd survived and now he would have a new life.

He took a bite of the sandwich. Slightly stale bread. Cucumber. A sweet and sticky mango chutney. He was starving.

He'd thought he would land in the USA. When he

paid Ameer to get him on the plane, he paid to go to the USA. But as soon as he landed and spoke to the woman, and looked around, and shook off the cramps in his legs, he realized he had landed in England. In Pakistan, Yacub thought, we love England but we also blame it for our problems, though not nearly as much as we love and blame the USA.

After he finished eating, he stood beside the door, listening. The house remained quiet. He tried to remember where to find the toilet. In the corridor on the way to the front door—that's right. A tiny below-stairs cubicle with a minute sink. He washed as best he could, bent over beneath the sloping ceiling, cleaning his face with soapy water. He needed to wash properly; he'd be able to think straight when he was clean. He decided to explore the house a little more.

But as he stepped out into the corridor he felt overwhelmingly tired yet again. He thought of Raheela; he had given her his phone before he left Karachi. He would find a way to phone her later today. He went back to his room and this time left the door ajar, climbed into the bed, and went straight back to sleep.

The next time he woke up, he could hear a gun battle.

5

Here was Jack at his happiest: in front of the TV with *World of Battle Fatigues* online, volume turned up so he could hear the Americans, who were also playing, talking to each other—Jack didn't use the headset to talk while he was playing but he liked to listen to the other players. "Fuck you," one American said. "Fuck that," another replied.

Given that it was the end of the afternoon in London, it must have been morning where they were, but the Americans seemed to be online all day and all night. The graphics of the game—a burnt-out landscape that nature was reclaiming—were hyperreal and the game was light on gore, which Jack preferred: he liked to gun down his opponents in cold blood but he didn't like to see them bleed. "Fuck you!" shouted the American. "Fuck that!" shouted another.

On Jack's right, at a ninety-degree angle to the TV, accessible with a simple swivel of his chair, was the coffee table where he had the following to hand: a snack, preferably something sweet; a drink—some kind of smoothie as Jack's mother wouldn't buy fizzy drinks; his phone, so he could message with his friends; and his laptop. He had YouTube open so that he could play music videos;

Facebook, with at least three, maybe even as many as fifteen chat windows open so he could chat with his friends in private; instant messaging as well so that all of his friends who were also online could join in the conversation, which mostly consisted of attempts to mimic the sound of their own farts through elaborate use of random fonts and keyboard symbols; one of the casual games sites Jack liked so that when the chat got boring and the texts stopped coming and his console was reloading he could race a car or two; Skype, in case he wanted to speak to someone face to face; and his Tumblr page so he could capture the best of it all for posterity. And his homework open in the background so when his mum came into the room he could show her what he was *really* doing.

So that's what Jack was doing that day, getting on with what he thought of as "my glorious stupid life." He was fiddling with his handset, wishing he could afford to buy some of the game's currency, and thinking about how there should be a law to Give Kids More Money. Then a man appeared beside him.

Jack was so startled he dropped the handset and fell backward to the floor.

At this, the strange man laughed.

Then the strange man extended his hand, offering to help Jack up. "I'm Yacub," he said. "I'm staying in the room at the back of the kitchen. Don't tell your mother you saw me."

"What the fuck?" Jack replied. He didn't usually swear out loud at home; he used his "at home" way of speaking.

But the stranger had a strong Middle Eastern–type accent that made Jack think of *24* and *Homeland* and a dozen other American shows and movies. Jack thought the strange man could definitely be a Very Bad Man—his trousers and shirt ragged and filthy, the way he stank of—what was it?—petrol and sweat, even if everything else about him— his manner, the way he was standing there in bare feet, the friendly look on his young face—said he wasn't.

"You are swearing at me," the man said.

Now Jack felt a wave of sympathy for him, followed quickly by a backwash of self-loathing. "No, no," he said, "not really *at* you, more *with* you."

The man waved his hand again, a little impatiently this time. Jack took it, and the man pulled him up from the floor. Jack thought that for a guy who was very skinny and five-five, maybe five-six at the most, he was strong. Jack himself was six-foot-five with the strength of a dandelion after it had gone to seed.

"You are Jack," the man said. "I'm Yacub," he said again. "I'm staying in the room behind the kitchen. You are a giant."

I'm a giant, and you're a little sprite. *Who the fuck are you?* Jack wanted to say. But instead, he said, "Why are you in my house?"

The man beckoned him to follow. He passed through the kitchen toward the room out back where the family kept stuff they no longer needed. Maybe he's a burglar, Jack thought, some kind of weird petrol-addict burglar who instead of taking your cash and jewelry, moves in.

But when the man opened the door to the room out back, Jack couldn't have been more surprised. It had been cleared and cleaned and turned into a neat little bedroom. Jack could see his mother's hand at work, down to the tidy curtains she probably told herself she would sew but ended up buying at the department store instead.

"Please don't tell your mother you can see me. She thinks I'm dead."

"Are you?"

Yacub raised his eyebrows. "Of course not."

Jack looked at Yacub. Yacub looked at Jack.

"And I would like to play the computer game with you," he added.

6

After Harriet lost her job, she concentrated mostly on the things she did badly: shopping for food, parenting Jack, cleaning the house, staying in shape, being married. Some of these things she did more badly than others— being married, for instance. She and Michael were both really crap at that. She reckoned she was probably most proficient at shopping for food, though even then, she was often mesmerized by the special offers and forgot the essentials.

For a while, Michael used to object to her endless trips to the supermarket. "Do you go every day?" he asked one evening, when he opened the fridge and discovered it was so full he had to struggle to close it again. "You've got better things to do."

"No I don't," she said.

He turned toward her as though to reply.

They stood in the kitchen, looking at each other. The room filled up with everything there was to say, all the arguments they hadn't had, all the explaining they hadn't done, all the anger, the guilt, the recriminations, and the apologies.

Jack walked in. "What can I eat?" he asked, although they'd finished supper less than an hour ago.

"An apple," Harriet said, and she went back to her computer. Michael went back to the TV.

Losing her job had been cataclysmic for Harriet. After she'd had Jack, she'd spent more than a decade feeling blurry and out of focus in the world, but she'd finally woken up and started to sharpen up, and then—bam!—it was over. The past two years had been lost to supermarket shopping.

Today her focus was on figuring out what to do about the car. After Jack left for school, Michael for work, she stood for a few moments outside Yacub's door, listening, before opening it as quietly as possible. He was sleeping soundly, snoring pleasantly. She left him a sandwich and a note. Then she walked to the supermarket and, once there, wandered around the car park trying to remember where the car was parked. A plane flew low overhead, coming in to land at Heathrow. Aha, a couple of rows of cars over, farther south. But the car was not there. She was stymied.

She remained long enough for three more airplanes to pass overhead. They lowered their landing gear at the same point and aimed for the runway. Harriet thought about how everyone inside the plane worried for a few seat-belted minutes until the aircraft hit the tarmac and leveled out. Then their worry was transformed into impatience.

She went into the supermarket to see if someone knew what had happened to her crumpled car.

7

Emily hadn't been out with anyone since she broke up with Harv. She knew she'd been cruel to Harv, but at the time she felt she'd had no alternative; they'd had a pretend relationship and the death of her father had made her see it for what it was—a little weird, a little damaging. Since then her friends had tried to set her up from time to time, but she wasn't interested. Work was always busy, and she had her film project, which her friends had taken to calling *Me, Myself, and I* because whenever they asked Emily what it was about, she'd say, "Oh, just me and some stuff I'm interested in." She turned down their offers of help—most of her friends worked in TV as well. They laughed at her, but she knew they also admired her a little. At least she was working on her own project, unlike most of them whose many ideas for zombie movies never got past the talking-about-it-in-the-pub phase.

Emily missed Harv, a little. He'd got involved with another girl immediately. She thought if they'd still been together she would have told him about her film project, about Harriet, and that, of all her friends, Harv would have understood what she was doing.

Her hair was a deep, dark shade of red, claret really, at the moment. Shooting had started the week before on

Ginger—a new reality show about a group of young people with red hair—and everyone in the production team
had dyed their hair for the first day of filming. In the
bathroom, she looked at herself in the mirror. She looked
even less like Harriet than before. There was no family
resemblance that she could detect. Emily had spent hours
spooling through her own footage, looking at Harriet
from every angle, close-up, right side, left side, from
behind—she had plenty of friends who looked nothing
like their mothers except when sighted from behind. But
there was nothing. Of course, she'd never actually spoken
to Harriet. You don't really know what someone is like
until you talk to them. Once they spoke to each other,
Emily knew everything would change.

The time to draw the filming to a close was approaching, Emily could feel it. She needed to finish the film
and get on with her life. The falling man would play a
part in this, though she still had no idea what that part
might be.

8

Jack didn't see much of his father these days. When times were good, Michael worked long hours to minimize risk and maximize profit. When times were bad, he worked long hours to minimize risk and maximize profit. His father didn't much like his job at Oldman Skanks, though Michael laughed when Jack called it that, and Jack had even heard Michael call it that himself. Michael was kind of old these days, and he was a bit fat, and Jack knew that he smoked when he was out for a drink in the City—cigars, most likely—and he wouldn't be surprised if his father keeled over dead one day, *phwump*, onto his desk. He was at that age, the right demographic. Last year Jack wrote a biology report about middle-aged men who drop dead from heart failure. He titled it "Oldman Skanks" and got a B. As for skanks, no, not his dad. As far as Jack knew, Michael had Harriet, and Harriet had Michael.

Gross. Disgusting. He didn't want to think about that. They'd had that rough patch a couple of years ago but nothing came of it. They were as married and as boring as always.

Michael and Jack had gone to the barber together on the weekend; they did this every six weeks or so. They always walked there. Jack would have preferred to drive, but his dad insisted. They talked about sports, which neither of them were all that interested in. When Jack was five, one day his dad had said, "We'd better pick a team. English boys need to support a football team."

"Manchester United," Jack had said. Some of his friends at school supported them. Frank had a miniature Manchester United kit that he wore most weekends.

"No," his dad said. "Let's go for a London team."

Jack couldn't think of any London teams.

"Let's support Chelsea," Michael said.

And so they did. Now as they walked to the barber, they discussed how the team was faring. Jack gleaned enough information from the internet to pretend he knew what he was talking about, while his father took a more statistics-based, analytical approach. That conversation didn't last long and they walked the rest of the way in silence. But the silence between them was easy. Unlike with Harriet. With his mum, Jack always felt as if she was barely keeping a lid on it, all the millions of things she wanted to say to him, all the instructions, all the questions. Sometimes he dreaded being with her.

Still, Jack got along better with his mum these days. Well, kind of. Sometimes. He thought that since they had their "events" and she lost her job, she had softened a little. No, that wasn't the right word. Acquiesced. Given up. She had more time. The domestic goddess routine didn't suit her, Jack and his mum both knew that, but they pretended. The fact was, Jack didn't need her anymore. In some countries he'd have left home ages ago. In some countries he'd have a job and a wife and a child of his own. Or he'd live in a slum and sell his body for crack. Jack wondered about Yacub. Maybe he had five kids and a wife in a burqa back in his village in Iraq or wherever he came from. Jack resolved to ask where he was from, maybe once they'd finished this game. Sometimes he wondered about leaving home, heading off into the wide blue yonder, but then he thought: no. Who would cook his dinner? Who would pay his allowance?

Being sixteen sucked: tons of exams and no money. Still, Jack told himself, it was better than being fifteen. And that was better than being fourteen. Fourteen was truly crap. When he was fourteen, David McDonald died and Ruby ended up in hospital and he might have been responsible; he nearly got expelled; he and his mum got chased by a psychopath and his mum lost her job. Fourteen sucked.

Yacub and Jack played *World of Battle Fatigues* for a while—Jack was surprised to find Yacub was pretty good at it for a guy who was living in the little room at the back of the house. He heard Harriet's keys in the front door.

"That's her," he said.

"Your mother?"

"She's coming in."

Yacub stood up and put his hands together and gave

Jack a little bow. "Very nice to have made your acquaintance," he said. "I'd better go."

He shut the door to the little room as Harriet entered the sitting room. Jack pretended to be playing his game.

"Hi," she said.

His mother sounded tired.

"Hi," he replied.

As always, his mum took the fact that Jack responded to her greeting to mean that he was ready for a full-on conversation. "How was your day?"

"Fine," Jack said. Ordinarily, he wouldn't pause the gameplay, but today he paused. "How about yours?"

She was carrying a shopping bag and a handful of paperwork. She went straight into the kitchen. Before Jack realized it, he'd followed her.

"Okay," she said. "A bit tiring."

He struggled to stop himself from firing a string of questions at her. Instead he tried to remember how he behaved normally: oh yeah, I ask her to do stuff for me. "Can you drive me to school in the morning? I've got to take back all that kit."

The color drained from his mother's face. She swallowed. "Can't," she said. "No car."

"Where's the car?" Jack asked.

His mother's eyes widened and her nostrils flared. Jack thought, It's as though I'm the parent and she's the truth-dodging teen. "I had an accident."

"What happened?"

She paused long enough to give herself away.

"A tree fell on the car."

He folded his arms across his chest. "Oh yeah?" he said. "Were you hurt?"

"No. I wasn't in the car at the time. It's in the garage. I'm waiting to hear whether it can be fixed."

He could see from her face that she had managed to move from lying into more truthful territory. But it didn't make sense. A tree fell on her car? How? Where?

"I'll cook supper later," she said. "Do you have any homework? Have you done your guitar?"

He rolled his eyes at her and slouched back into the sitting room.

Most days when Jack and Harriet were home together he was either in his room on his laptop or in front of the games console, and she was in the kitchen at her so-called workstation. Harriet had spent a large part of the past two years online—doing what, she was never quite sure, given the way time contracted on the internet. She monitored news stories and had become fascinated with the way that certain stories started as tiny specks but then became huge sandstorms, like the way a young man immolating himself in Tunisia became the Arab Spring.

The kitchen computer corner now resembled the NASA control room at Houston—three big monitors, two keyboards, a couple of smartphones, several tablets, an e-reader, an external hard drive, a backup drive, and a small jungle's worth of cables. Occasionally, very occasionally, Jack brought his laptop into the kitchen with him and they worked together companionably. One afternoon a while back, Harriet got up to make dinner and was standing behind Jack at the counter. She could see his screen over his shoulder. He had his headphones on with at least a dozen windows open at the same time—he was watching music videos and using chat and a bunch of other applications and websites that Harriet had never seen before. It was unusual, this opportunity to watch him online, and as she chopped the onion she tried to act normally, so that he didn't cotton on to the fact that she was spying on him. Now that he was a bit older he seemed to find her slightly less annoying, but if he noticed her watching him, she'd be in trouble.

So she had watched him as he flicked from site to site, conversation to conversation. He moved rapidly, looking at his friends' photos, responding to their comments. He was happy. Harriet was happy. She chopped that onion for ages, all the way through the very loud Skype discussion with his friend about the merits of Frank Ocean or otherwise.

But today Jack was on his games console in the sitting room and Yacub was in the little room out back. Yacub seemed okay. She'd checked on him just now—asleep again under the heaped-up covers, but the sandwich had been eaten.

What was she going to do with him? How was she going to tell Michael and Jack that a man fell from a plane onto her car and she'd brought him home? There was no point in telling anyone anything if Yacub was in fact dead. Do ghosts eat sandwiches? Had no one else seen him fall?

She used all three of the screens simultaneously, flicking through the feeds and the alerts. She was usually very precise with keywords, search terms, and hashtags, but now she threw the net wider and wider: landing gear, Heathrow, #Pakistan, asylum, illegal entry, supermarket car parks, #fallingmen, man falling, flight paths, sky. Nothing—well, plenty of stuff surfaced but she did not find any references or links to her falling man, however oblique. She kept poking away, moving from application to application, website to website, search engine to search engine, new media to old media. Nothing.

Jack came into the kitchen. "When's supper?" he asked.

"I'm about to start cooking. It'll be quick."

Jack nodded. "Supermarket special," he said approvingly. Normally he would shuffle off at this point: he had to shuffle because he wore his trousers slung so low he walked with his legs spread wide apart. But this time he didn't walk away. Instead he stood there, looming over Harriet.

"What are you doing?"

She looked up at him. He was peering at the screens, and Harriet could see he was actually interested, which in and of itself was peculiar and worrying.

"Nothing," she said.

"Nothing?" he asked.

Harriet looked back at the screens. He couldn't possibly figure out what she was doing—what happened yesterday.

And then she saw it. There was a message in one of the streams: "Is it a plane? Is it a bird? Or is it a man, falling?" followed by a crunched photo URL.

Harriet suppressed a gasp by pretending to clear her throat. "I bought some of those Belgian waffle biscuits you like—they're in the cupboard," she said, knowing that nothing could be interesting enough to divert Jack from biscuits.

"Yum." He hoicked up his trousers and ambled to the cupboard.

Once he was gone, she clicked on the link.

A photo of a man, falling, indistinct yet unmistakable. A cloudless day, an empty sky. The airplane Yacub had fallen from already out of the frame, so it was as though he was falling from Heaven itself, an angel without wings.

Whoever took it was not in the supermarket car park, she could tell, but a distance away. Harriet enlarged the photo, disturbing the pixels, making the whole thing even more blurry. There was the roof of the supermarket. There was the main road to the bridge. The photographer was somewhere above ground level, maybe two or three floors up, in a block of flats or offices perhaps, looking south. She opened the map on her tablet and watched the globe spin round before she used the touchscreen to find her virtual way to the supermarket. She'd figure out where the photo was taken from. And then what would she do?

Someone else saw Yacub falling.

Harriet was not sure why she felt compelled to keep Yacub's presence in the house a secret. She knew it was not a good idea. But Harriet was a keeper of secrets; keeping secrets was something she excelled at. She had never told Michael about Emily. By the time they met, keeping that secret had become second nature to her. It was something that nestled inside her, kicking her sharply in the ribs from time to time. Soon it was too late for it to be anything other than a shocking revelation, so it remained a secret. She kept secrets from Jack too, as parents do, all the smoking and drinking and drug taking and inappropriate sex with the wrong men at the wrong time in her past. Her dread fear of losing him, her terror that he wouldn't love her when she was old: she kept those secret, of course. It was not difficult to keep secrets from Jack. It hadn't occurred to him yet that his parents had lived lives of their own.

All in all, Harriet was a fan of secrets, and she wished Michael had seen fit to keep what happened in Toronto to himself. But she had guessed and he had confirmed her guess, as though he expected to be forgiven simply for having told the truth. But she hadn't forgiven him, not really. And now that was a secret too. So, not telling her husband and her son about Yacub was perfectly reasonable. How do you tell someone that a man fell out of the sky and onto your car, like a Pakistani David Bowie, and that you felt compelled to bring him home with you and hide him, even though you weren't entirely sure if he was dead or alive?

After she recovered from the shock of finding the photo, Harriet cooked. She had long since banned the use of laptops and phones during dinner, and neither she nor Jack broke that rule often. Once they were sitting together at the table, she would try to start a conversation, which was never easy. Like his father, Jack wasn't much of a talker. Harriet's attempts at light and breezy teatime conversation rarely succeeded and—she tried to stop herself but was unable—their discussion usually deteriorated into a series of pointed questions about Jack's homework, his social plans, and his friends, none of which he wanted to discuss. But she kept trying anyway.

"Do you have any plans for the weekend?"

"Don't know."

"How's your essay going?"

"Okay."

"How is Ruby?"

"Don't really see her these days, not since she switched schools."

They had gone through phases where talking was easier. When she lost her job, it became apparent that Jack was worried the family would no longer have enough money to stay in the big house, to keep taking holidays, so they'd talked about that a fair amount. There was plenty of money, and as long as Michael kept working there would continue to be plenty of money. They also spent a lot of time discussing the "events" that had led to Harriet's losing her job, which was understandable given that Jack was with her when it happened, though she lied about George Sigo—one more secret—claiming she had no idea who he was. Other allowable topics included Jack's elaborate critiques of Harriet's cooking, as though they were on *The Great British Bake Off*, Harriet a hapless competitor and Jack an exacting judge. But apart from that, Harriet and Jack lived their lives so separately that there was nothing to discuss. They didn't even watch TV together—Jack watched what he wanted on his laptop, and Harriet watched what she wanted on her tablet in bed. Michael worked late, came home, and left for work early the next day.

Harriet had spent the day trying to sort out the car. It had been impounded and towed away and it took her hours to track it down. She didn't want to talk to Jack about that. And there was the ghost of Yacub in the little room. She didn't want to talk about that either. Plus the photo she'd found online. With all these hidden things pressing in on her, tonight she decided to take the easy way out and opted for silence.

"So," Jack said, "how's the job hunt?"

She could not remember the last time he had started a conversation voluntarily.

"Well," she said, trying not to sound too pleased, "not so great. I mean, it's tough out there. Plus I'm past my sell-by date. I've expired."

Jack laughed and she laughed too; she was filled with happiness because he had shown an interest in her.

"Past your sell-by date. Come on, no you're not."

"I am, actually. Who wants to employ a middle-aged woman who has been out of work for two years and who was sacked from her last job?"

"You weren't sacked."

Harriet took a deep breath. "I might as well have been."

"Are you even looking?"

That was the kind of loaded, not-very-nice question that Harriet was prone to ask Jack, like "Are you even bothering to revise your paper?" She was startled to think he'd learned the technique from her. She took another gulp of air. "You're right. I suppose I have given up looking."

"You should volunteer."

"I've got enough on my plate, taking care of you and your dad."

Harriet thought about the empty, immaculate house.

They finished eating and Harriet cleared. Jack retreated to his bedroom with his laptop. She waited for a while to make sure he was thoroughly ensconced. Then she knocked as quietly as she could on Yacub's door.

Yacub looked the same as the last time Harriet had seen him awake. But now, she noticed, he smelled. Harriet recognized the smell: it was like stepping outside the terminals at Heathrow—jet engine fuel. He wouldn't have had a chance to wash properly since he arrived, and Harriet felt bad for not thinking of that earlier. The hearty pong made her feel relieved; if he was dead, he wasn't likely to be suffering from body odor. However, if he was alive, maybe he needed to pray, but he couldn't pray if he wasn't clean. And god knows which direction Mecca might be.

"I'm sorry, I should have shown you the bathroom. It's upstairs. You'll want to take a shower or have a bath. And I've saved you some supper."

"Food first, bath later, please, Mrs. Harriet."

"Just Harriet is fine," she replied.

While Yacub ate, she went upstairs and ran the bath. She called out to Jack, "I'm having a bath," but the volume of his music did not go up or down. Once Yacub finished eating and was in the bath, she knocked on Jack's door and went in. He turned the volume down and looked at her.

"Do you have any clothes that are too small? I'm doing a big sort-through."

"I thought you were in the bath."

She could feel she was blushing. "I ran it, but then I thought I'd do this first."

Without a word of objection, Jack disentangled himself from his wires and leads and cables and went over to his chest of drawers. He got out a pair of tracksuit bottoms and two T-shirts. "These are too small. Most of my clothes are too small," he said.

The unmistakable sound of someone readjusting their position in the bathtub—*brraap, slosh*—came through the wall. Jack and Harriet stared at each other. Harriet held her breath. But then Jack made his way back to his bed and his computer, his sound system, and his phone, as though he hadn't heard a thing.

She took the clothes into her room, added a sweater of her own, wrote a note for Yacub, pushed the note under the bathroom door, and left the clothes outside the door in a bag.

10

Yacub was planning to leave that night. He'd decided to make his own way in London; he didn't need any more help from this woman with her wide face and her ready smile and her son who was both gigantic and babyish. He wanted to get out of their house and find work and make his way, like he did in Karachi, like he did in Dubai. He'd earn enough money to fly to America, this time inside the cabin of a plane.

But the bath was his downfall. It was the biggest, most wonderful bath he had ever been in. Actually, it was the only bath he had ever been in. When he first climbed into it, he was astonished. Warm water, up to his shoulders. Bubbles that smelled of perfume. The smooth surface to lie back against. The cool air on his face. The solitude. The peace.

The bath melted his resolve. Everything was white in the room—white walls, white tiles, white-painted floorboards, white toilet, big white chair, white blind on the large window, a separate glass-walled shower in the corner, everything lined up, square, no cracks, no holes, no rats, no insects, no escaping sewage—it was like a bathroom in a magazine, an American bathroom in an American magazine. Harriet had put out two thick white towels, a white bar of soap, and a new toothbrush. The toothbrush was green.

And it was in that bath, in the extreme comfort of that bath, that Yacub realized his body hurt all over. He was still cold, still frozen deep in his core. He could do with another night of rest in that clean, soft bed.

He would leave the house tomorrow.

11

Michael came home from work late and left for work early every day; the bed he shared with Harriet was so wide and firm that no end of people could have come and gone, leaving Harriet's sleep unbroken. Besides, she was tired. When Jack became a teenager, his newfound passion for late nights had the opposite effect on her, rendering her unable to stay awake past ten o'clock.

Harriet tried to stay up. She missed her husband, as though he'd been away at sea for a long time and she had no idea when he'd return. And yet most nights, if she was awake when he came into the bedroom, she pretended to be asleep. Two years was a long time to go without talking. Who knew where "Hello, how are you?" might lead?

They weren't "not talking" in the cold-shouldered sense. They could sit at a dinner table together and converse about Jack, Michael's work, the news, the weather.

Of course, when the "events" happened, Michael had asked her about George Sigo, and she had lied. But had she? No, she just hadn't told him the whole truth. She resigned from her job, emailing an apology to Mallory. She didn't see how she could continue to work after what had happened; she thought that every time she appeared on television or radio, that scene—Harriet in her suit in front of the candidates, the mayor of Tipton Mallet behind her on the stage, George pushing her into Frankenstein—would replay in the mind of the audience, and that no one would ever again hear what she was trying to report. The "events" allowed Michael to stand by his wife, steadfast. They had allowed them both to push away what had happened in Toronto.

They had survived. And then Yacub arrived: at last something new was happening to Harriet's family.

It wasn't much of a family. Two parents, one child—well short of the 2.4 required for the next generation to thrive.

Once Yacub was out of the bath and safely back in his room, Harriet found herself unable to sit still and so began to clean shelves, sort towels, throw out old food. When Jack was younger and Harriet worked, she had done none of these things: the cleaner sorted, the nanny cooked. Now, to keep herself company while she pottered in the kitchen, she went online and found a Pakistani cookery show, with a flamboyant male chef in a hot-pink shirt, speaking a weird mix of what she took to be Urdu and English, busy making some kind of sugary rice pudding. Harriet wondered if she should try to make it.

After the kitchen was tidy, the floor swept and washed, the rubbish taken out, she headed off to bed. Yacub was in the little room, and even Jack seemed to have had an early night. She turned out the light on her bedside table and lay in the dark, illuminated by the cold, clean light of her tablet. She went on Facebook, logging on under her other identity, Crazeeharree, going straight to Emily's page. New pictures. Harriet sighed with satisfaction.

After a while, she pressed a button and the tablet fell dark and the room was dark as well. Harriet lay back on her pillow and listened to the house. The digital clock read 00:15; Michael was later than usual.

She dozed. Tomorrow she'd take Yacub shopping and buy him clothes. Did he need more clothes? All he possessed were the filthy and tattered clothes on his back, and the hand-me-downs from Jack. If he was dead, that was one thing, but if he was alive, he would need proper clothes. They'd go over to the giant mall in Shepherd's Bush and she'd take him to the men's shops—or maybe she should give him the money and let him shop for himself—oh lord, she thought, complicated. Maybe she'd hand him the money and he'd disappear in the crowd and that would be it. The car would come back from the garage and the little room out back would once again fill up with stuff they didn't need. It would be as though Yacub had never existed.

Harriet slept, until she was woken by the sound of Michael entering the room. She listened as he took off his clothes, placing everything carefully on the sofa by the window, sitting down on the bed to remove his shoes. He took off his cuff links and they clinked as he put them on the bedside table. He climbed into bed and took a deep breath. These were sounds that Harriet had heard thousands of times, but tonight she heard them afresh. He was being as quiet as he could possibly be. He was a considerate man.

Then he did the unexpected: he began to move toward her. He knew she was awake. He glided across the expanse of their bed like a swimmer moving toward the shore. She had her back to him, and he slid his hand over her hip and pulled her close. She could smell the soap that he had washed with and the toothpaste he had used, and behind that the alcohol he had consumed that evening. He was tangy with the office and train on him still. They hadn't had sex since he'd been to Toronto. He put his hand on her hip, and he moved ever closer. He was kissing her neck and her back, pressing himself against her.

She turned to face him. He brought his face close for a kiss. He lifted her leg and pulled her to him.

Harriet put her hands on her husband's chest and gave him a great, heavy shove. She pushed him roughly again, and again, and again, and he grunted each time her hands landed on his chest, air whooshing from his lungs, his head snapping forward as she pushed him across the bed. As she pushed, she thought, Poor man, he works long hours at a difficult job and this is what he gets. He didn't deserve it. But that didn't stop her from pushing him so hard that eventually she pushed him completely out of the bed. He hit his head on the sharp edge of the bedside table on his way to the floor.

"Ouch!" he said. "Harriet."

She scuttled like a crab back to her side of the bed, turned over, and snuggled down as though Michael was not back from work, was not in the house, let alone the bedroom.

"Harriet," he said, his tone less surprised and a bit harsher this time. "Harriet." Now he sounded angry. She heard him sit up and rub his head. "Ouch," he said again, and she was reminded of the overpriced dancing robot they'd bought Jack one Christmas. It fell over all the time and would mournfully say "Ouch" before being set upright to resume dancing. Michael got up, pulled on a T-shirt and some underwear and his dressing gown, and left.

Harriet remained in bed. What just happened? What would happen next? She hadn't realized how angry she was. She'd got used to the way they lived, she got on with things, Jack got on with things, Michael worked long hours and they'd given up living a normal family life years and years and years ago. What was a normal family like anyway? She loved him. And she'd pushed him out of bed and onto the floor.

The house remained quiet. She heard the toilet flush. She heard Michael make his way down the stairs.

Then, moments later, at the same moment that Harriet thought, *Oh no, Yacub*, Michael began shouting.

12

Despite the lovely warm bath and the thick soft towels and the clean, perfect bed, Yacub could not sleep. Each time he closed his eyes it would happen again: with an enormous clunk and whirr, the landing gear began to unfold itself in front of him, the great pistons and wheels moving into place, the stink of fuel and oil and machinery. Caught off guard, off balance, dizzy, frozen, only half conscious, afraid, he toppled from the shelf where he'd been trapped, crouching for hours and hours, and was cast out into the limitless sky, the ground rushing toward him much too quickly. And then he'd wake with a shout and a flail, landing in the clean, perfect bed, the most comfortable bed in the world. After what felt like hours, he gave up and resigned himself to lying there, awake.

He was beginning to fall asleep once again when the door to the room opened and light flooded in from the kitchen. In the door stood a man, not as tall as Jack and much heavier. Yacub knew immediately that he was the father of the household and that the father had come to kill him.

The man turned on the overhead light. At first it was as though he didn't notice Yacub, as though he was looking for something else. But then the words rushed from his mouth: "What the fuck . . . who the fuck . . . what are you . . . ?"

Yacub bolted from the bed. He threw back the curtains and tried to lever open the window. But it was heavy and in his panic it stuck. He turned, grabbed the wooden chair and wielded it over his head like a weapon, hoping the father was not armed.

"Put that down!" Michael bellowed. He stepped toward Yacub, who realized that if the man came any closer he was going to have to bring the chair down on his head.

Then Mrs. Harriet arrived, shrieking.

Pakistan is a hard country, quick to humiliate or otherwise destroy the wise, placing its profoundest hopes in fools. Yacub first decided to leave when he was a small boy and saw his fate mapped out for him by his father, and the alternatives on the television in the village café. But this decision, which led him away from his family, first to Karachi, then to Dubai, and now here, caused him pain. His father's village, high in the mountain valley, had not fared well over the past decade. The men with beards. The Americans. The drones. The army. And the earthquake, followed a few years later by the floods. Nobody takes their holidays in the mountain valleys anymore. There was nothing there for Yacub. He'd spent four months in a bankrupted Dubai labor camp. He'd spent hours crushed on a freezing shelf at thirty thousand feet. And now, an angry *gora* was about to kill him.

He put the chair back down and sat on it. He was ready. It was time to die.

13

When Jack woke and heard the shouting, he assumed the worst, which, even though he was sixteen now and could in theory fend for himself, was that his mum and dad were having an enormous row and were splitting up and he'd have to choose between them.

But then he heard the noise was coming from the kitchen. Yacub, he thought. And Dad. Shit.

By the time he got down the stairs, his mother was trying to calm down his dad. Yacub was sitting in a chair, looking miserable and skinny, as though he'd rather go back to Afghanistan or wherever and be recruited by the Taliban than be stuck here with Jack's lousy family.

"He landed on my car," Harriet was saying, "in the supermarket car park."

Of course. Where else?

His father stared at his mother.

"I thought he was dead."

"Well, he's not dead," his father said, categorically.

Jack and Harriet both looked at Yacub. He definitely wasn't dead. Jack felt a bit foolish for believing even a tiny bit that he might be.

"I'm not dead," Yacub confirmed, though he sounded as though he wished he was or thought he would be soon.

"I wasn't sure," said Harriet. "He needed help. He needs us."

"What?" said Jack's dad. "Who is he? A refugee?"

"No—he—"

"You're moving strangers into the house without even telling me?"

Jack noticed that his father was bleeding from a cut on the top of his head. Blood had snaked through what was left of his hair and was making its way across his forehead. Had Yacub hit him? Jack felt an unfamiliar surge of anger; he couldn't just stand by, yet again, when his parents were under threat. And he'd liked the guy! He pushed past his mother and into the little room and threw himself at Yacub, wrestling him off the chair and onto the floor.

"Jack!" Harriet shrieked. "Stop it!"

Jack expected Yacub to put up a fight, but he lay there on the floor without moving. Jack had him pinned down by the shoulders. Yacub looked up at Jack with an expression of such weariness that Jack stopped, confused.

"You didn't have to hit my dad!" Jack said. "He's an old guy."

"Jack," Michael said, "he didn't hit me. Your mother did."

"I did not!"

Michael sighed. "Let's just say it was an injury from a previous incident that took place earlier this evening."

"You're bleeding," said Harriet, and she moved toward her husband with a tissue from her dressing gown pocket, but he stopped her before she could touch him. He took the tissue out of her hand without touching her.

"Thank you," he said, sounding oddly formal. "I'll take care of it myself."

Jack stood up and offered a hand to help Yacub off the floor. "Sorry," he said. Yacub took his hand and sat down on the bed.

"I suppose he is," Harriet said.

"Is what?" asked Michael.

"A kind of refugee."

"I'm not a refugee," Yacub said sharply. "I've come to work. I'm not staying in this country. I'm going to America."

Michael snorted.

"You're going to the US?" Jack asked. He wasn't sure why, but he felt like crying. Luckily he had learned how not to cry two years back. "Who will play *World of Battle Fatigues* with me?" he asked, immediately regretting it— pathetic whinger.

"You've met?" Harriet asked. "You've played games?"

"You can't hide someone in our house and expect me not to notice," Jack replied. "It's my house too. I live here."

"Okay," his mother said. "Let's go back to bed. We'll talk this through in the morning."

So that's what they did. They all went back to bed.

Jack couldn't sleep. So he did what he always did when he couldn't sleep: he thought about Dukes Meadows on a sunny summer's day, and he thought about Ruby.

14

Harriet listened to Michael breathing, knowing he was listening to her.

After a while, she spoke into the darkness of the room. "He's just a boy."

"Where'd you get him from?"

"You make it sound like I *bought* him at the super-market."

"Harriet, who is he and what is he doing here?"

"We'll talk tomorrow, Michael."

"I'll be home late. I've got a meeting."

"On a Friday night?"

"There are people here from New York. I have to be there."

"Of course."

They stopped talking and rolled over, away from each other. They pretended to fall asleep for so long, they fell asleep.

In the morning, as usual, Michael was gone before either Harriet or Jack was up. Jack announced that when he got home from school he would take Yacub shopping for clothes. "I'll introduce him to the joys of British high street shopping," he said. "I'll take him for coffee and load him up with the latest stuff."

"Okay," said Harriet, relieved at the thought that she wouldn't have to do this herself. "Great."

"You'll need to give me cash," Jack said. "Lots."

He packed the sandwich she had made him and left.

There was no sign of Yacub; she would leave him to sleep. Harriet took a shower, dressed, and got ready to walk down to the cash machine. She would go to the supermarket later, maybe while the boys—she laughed to herself at that, "the boys"—were out shopping. As she emerged from her house, she noticed the young woman on a bicycle across the street. As always she was stationary, one foot on the ground. She was staring straight ahead, as though waiting for an invisible traffic light to turn green.

Harriet never got a really good look at the girl on the bike; she wore a helmet, sunglasses, scarves. For a while Harriet thought she must be a new neighbor, but she knew most of her neighbors—their large terraced houses were underoccupied and overrenovated, like hers—and no one had moved in or out. Perhaps the girl was staying in the house across the street, though Harriet doubted that the retired circuit judge was the sort to let out rooms. From time to time Harriet wondered if the cyclist could in fact be Emily, but then thought it was too unlikely, couldn't be.

It looked like it might rain, so Harriet went back inside to get an umbrella, and when she came out again the girl was gone.

15

Every morning Michael walked to the station to take the train to work. The train to Waterloo, followed by the Drain into the City. He liked his commute, truth be told—it was a blank space between home and work. He left early and came home late so he avoided the crowds. He did his commute empty-handed—there weren't enough hours left in the day for him to have to work at home, so he didn't carry paperwork. He didn't read the newspaper, he didn't do email, he didn't shuffle through documents, he didn't fiddle with his phone; he walked, he sat, he looked out the window, he watched his fellow commuters, and he thought about nothing. It was a forty-minute meditation at each end of the day. It kept him from going crazy.

Michael was at a loss. He'd spent the last two years at a loss. He had no idea how to make amends to his wife; he wasn't in the habit of making amends simply because he was not in the habit of doing wrong. He thought perhaps—was it possible?—he'd never done anything wrong before in his entire life. No, he must have done something wrong at some point. But maybe not. He handed in wallets and umbrellas to lost property, he offered his seat on the train to older people, his expense account was pristine. He wasn't a big talker, so he'd never had occasion to exaggerate or, indeed, lie. He liked the same bands he'd listened to as a student, even when their reunion albums were lousy. When the Occupy people had been camped in front of St. Paul's, he bought them food and donated money, even though what they were protesting against in their vague, all-embracing way was him. Well, not him directly—he wasn't a banker—but his friends. Except, he corrected himself again, he didn't have any friends, he'd never been a person who made friends. His colleagues.

If there is an advantage to leaving where you come from and making your life somewhere new, it is that you can leave your past behind. Michael had left his past behind. He'd wobbled that time in Toronto, he'd allowed a combination of nostalgia and cocktails to morph into desire. But he'd left that behind as well.

The disadvantage to leaving where you come from and making your life somewhere new is that once enough years have passed, the new place is no longer new, and you find yourself burdened with a past after all. Michael had a long history in London; he'd lived in London for more years than he'd lived anywhere else. And he coped with this by becoming absent. He was absent from his family; he was absent from his life. He was the Man Who Wasn't There, except he *was* there, eating and working and taking the train into work every day. Going to meetings. Moving figures around spreadsheets. Estimating and assessing risk while remaining truly risk-averse himself.

And he had let people down. He had done wrong. To Harriet. Jack as well.

And now Harriet had invited a stranger into their house. Was this his punishment? A man who fell out of the sky?

16

On his way to school Jack thought about Yacub. Now that he was allowed to leave the little room out back and go into the world like a real person, not a ghost, Jack was looking forward to showing him round. After we've been to the shops, he thought, we'll visit the supermarket. It would be like a visit to Mecca for Yacub, Jack reckoned, or maybe not Mecca, since Yacub might be an actual Muslim and that might offend him. While out, they'd watch the planes lower their landing gear. He'd get Yacub to tell him what it was like to fall out of a plane. Jack could take him to the multiplex. He'd like that. And he could take him over the river to Dukes Meadows.

When Jack was fourteen, he and his friends fell into the habit of meeting at Dukes. But then David McDonald died. It all came to an abrupt end. Jack had handed the bag of weed to Ruby. It contained three little tablets. He saw Ruby take one. David McDonald probably took one. David McDonald died. Jack carried this knowledge around with him like an extra limb he kept hidden under his hoodie.

He kept track of Ruby and Frank on Facebook, but it wasn't the same as seeing them every day at school. Ruby was probably still down at Dukes with her cartwheels and her older brother who Jack had never spoken to but who, he felt sure, was as terrifying as ever.

While Jack was suspended, his mother had insisted on taking him with her that night she was covering the election, the night they got into trouble with George Psycho. The "events" changed Jack. Changed Jack and his mother. It was pretty spectacular, the video of her moment in front of the cameras, and it had a perpetual afterlife online. Jack sometimes watched it to remind himself that it really did happen, that he hadn't made it up. He had been standing behind the cameraman in the drafty town hall, watching the live broadcast, almost ready to admit that it was pretty interesting to watch his mum on TV. The producer with her clipboard, the candidates lined up on the stage, the ballot boxes, the party workers, all the purposeful activity. It took only a few moments—the man brushed by him on his way toward the stage. He ran straight for Jack's mum, he grabbed her and knocked her off her feet, and they slammed into the row of politicians behind them, and everyone fell, like dominoes, *clack, clack, clack.* His mother had shrieked when George Sigo grabbed her, and that shriek was lodged in Jack's brain, would always be.

It was strange to think about his mother losing everything in that moment. She wasn't hurt, not physically; only the guy dressed as Frankenstein was injured, and that was just a bang to the back of his head. The fact was, Jack was glad he had been there with his mum; he was glad she had not been alone that night. He was glad he witnessed what happened to her with his own eyes, not on YouTube, not on Facebook where, beneath the video, thousands of people had clicked on "Like."

When Jack got home from school, Yacub was in the sitting room watching TV; it was no longer necessary for him to hide. Jack felt a pang—he kind of missed having a strange man hiding in the little room out back. Harriet was in the kitchen baking a tart for dinner. Once Jack got out of his school uniform, cleaned himself up, and put on his newest jeans and his favorite T-shirt and a ton of cologne—you can never wear too much cologne—he was ready to head out to the shops with Yacub. His mother handed him a wedge of money. He looked at her in amazement.

"Two *hundred* pounds? You never give *me* this kind of money. Can I buy something for myself?"

"No," she said. "You can have a drink and a cake somewhere."

He was aware that Yacub had walked into the kitchen and was standing behind him, and he imagined what Yacub was thinking. Yes, Jack thought, I'm spoiled, I'm a fucking spoiled only child, but it's *her* fault, she's the one who spoiled me. He didn't look at Yacub.

"Yacub has nothing, remember. He needs underwear. He needs socks. He needs pajamas."

"Mrs. Harriet, I have no shoes," Yacub said.

"He needs shoes, he needs T-shirts and trousers and— He has nothing."

They both turned to look at him. He was wearing Jack's old track pants and an old sweater of Harriet's; somehow, he looked almost stylish.

"Mrs. Harriet, I have no shoes."

"He needs shoes," Harriet said.

"No," Yacub said, and Jack thought, Why, why does he keep repeating the same thing? "Excuse me, but you don't understand. I have no shoes now. They must have come off when I"—he paused, frowning, thinking—"disembarked from the plane."

"Oh," Jack and his mum both said, and they looked at his feet, which were indeed shoeless, plus Jack noticed he had a hole in one of his socks.

"Oh my god," said Harriet. "I'm so sorry."

There was no way that any of Jack's shoes would fit him. Jack was a giant with a giant's feet. Michael's were nearly as big. Harriet went to the cupboard near the front door and foraged, returning with a bunch of shoes, mostly her own old trainers. She made Yacub sit down and she lined up the shoes in front of him and they watched as he tried them on, one pair at a time, both of them willing the shoes to fit, as though he were Cinderella and Harriet and Jack his collective Prince.

And he was lucky. Even though Harriet was several inches taller than him, a pair of her old black Chucks fit, at least well enough to enable him to walk over to the high street with Jack to buy proper footwear.

"Thank you, Mrs. Harriet," Yacub said.

"It's nothing," she said. "We'll get you some shoes that actually fit properly. Please, call me Harriet."

"I will pay you back, Mrs. Harriet," he said, and he sounded both earnest and anxious. "Harriet," he corrected himself. Jack looked at him and thought, Shit, this can't be much fun for him, he's a grown man, not a lousy teenager like me, happy to live off my mum's handouts.

"I know you will," Harriet said, and she smiled.

So Jack walked him through the leafy streets, past the big houses, watching him as he looked around, wondering what he saw.

"Everything is green," Yacub said.

"It rains a lot," Jack replied.

"It's cold," he said. "It is very cold in England."

"This is warm, mate," Jack said. "Let's start by getting you a jacket."

It was like taking an alien shopping. Each time they went into a new shop, Yacub paused on the threshold. He took a good look around before entering. Jack had no idea why he did this. He himself headed right in and wandered around looking at stuff. Yacub caught up eventually. Jack didn't know if Yacub had ever been in shops like this before; he seemed startled by the idea of a fitting room. "You try things on first to make sure they look good," Jack said. "Then you take them off, put your own clothes back on, and pay." Yacub found a few things he liked and he actually seemed kind of excited when they went into the next shop.

"The colors," he said, "are nice. The clothes look," he paused again, "American."

He said the word *American* with such relish that Jack found it hard not to laugh.

"That's because they *are* American," he said.

Jack didn't often go into any of these stores because he was too tall to fit most of the clothes; he bought stuff online from specialty websites. Also, this particular shop was not cool, so ordinarily Jack wouldn't go near it. But Yacub was excited and that made Jack happy. I'm a good host, he thought. I'll have to remember to tell Mrs. Harriet. That woman underestimates me.

Jack was standing near the entrance to the fitting rooms, taking care of Yacub's bags while he tried things on, when Ruby walked through the doors.

She was standing in front of a table full of pastel-colored cardigans. She moved toward the shelves of jeans. The shop was not busy so Jack's view of her was clear. He hadn't run into her for several months, which was about a decade in teenager time, but she looked the same. Maybe her hair was a bit longer. Ruby had one of those bodies that made you turn away with embarrassment—it was so perfect. Everything tiny except the bits that were big. Her clothes were always exactly right, her hair, her lips, the way she smelled, the way she laughed, the way she . . . Jack hoped Yacub stayed in the fitting room forever so he could stand there for the rest of his life staring at Ruby without her noticing.

Ruby began to move through the shop toward him.

Jack was not sure what to do. She glanced around a few times as though she was looking for someone, but she didn't see Jack. This happened quite often. People did not notice Jack. Jack had a theory that he was too tall for people to see. On first glance he didn't register as human. People thought he was a tree. Or a lamppost. He kept watching her and as he watched, he saw her take one of the pastel cardigans she'd been looking at and slip it into her handbag. Then she made her way toward the fitting rooms. And, at long last, she saw him.

"Jack!" she said. "Hey."

"Hey," he said, "Ruby."

She put her hand on his arm and gave him a kiss on the cheek. Yacub chose that moment to come out of the fitting room. He looked at them. Then Jack watched his eyes widen as he took in Ruby, her shorts and her top, her hair, her eyes, and her lips. *I bet they don't make them like this where you come from!* Jack wanted to shout, but he managed not to do that, because of course they probably did make them like that where Yacub came from, they were just a little more covered up maybe.

"This is Yacub," he said to Ruby. He felt compelled to explain further, so he said the first thing that came to him: "He's my cousin. From the Pakistani side of my family."

"Cool," Ruby said. "Hi." And she held out her hand to him.

17

Yacub found the shopping trip with Jack overwhelming. It was not like him to find anything overwhelming. In Karachi the lady of the household took him shopping with her; she needed a peon to carry for her. The driver took them to the Forum, which was the brightest, slickest, shiniest place he had ever seen. They drove past the banks of sandbags and the guards in their towers with their machine guns, right up to the main entrance. Of course, once he got to Dubai he saw shops that were bigger and brighter and slicker and much more shiny, but he never actually entered any of those. So Richmond High Street made him display his amazement, something he was not comfortable doing. And Jack carried his bags.

And they met the girl called Ruby. Yacub had never met a girl dressed like Ruby, though of course he had seen them, in the distance in Dubai as the workers' bus took them past hotels and beaches, and on television. Even the girls in Imran's hotel dressed more modestly. Ruby shook his hand. Her face was open and friendly; she had this wide, happy smile with a small gap between her perfect white teeth. It was as though she generated her own supply of electricity, the air around her crackled and popped, and Yacub could see that Jack was drawn to her, that when she entered a room most men would have to look at her at least twice—once to see her, the second time to make sure she was real.

As they stood there, Ruby and Jack chatting, Yacub noticed three young men standing nearby. They were Pakistani, but they were not like any Pakistanis he'd ever seen before. They were dressed in low-slung, tight jeans and short, tight jackets, with big watches and gold neck chains, their hair gelled and slicked and styled. Punjabi, Yacub thought, though they were speaking a kind of messed-up Urdu—not Yacub's first language but one that he spoke, of course. Then they switched to English.

"Look at her," one said.

"I'd like to tap that," the other said.

"He's a freak, though," the third one said, nodding at Jack.

Then they all looked at Yacub. They could see that he was listening.

"Fuck you, Paki," one of them said. "Yeah, fuck you," another one said, and they laughed. They left the shop and went out into the street.

Jack and Ruby finished their conversation and Ruby gave Jack a kiss on the cheek, and she shook Yacub's hand once again. "Is this your first time in London?"

Yacub nodded.

"Well, have a great time. Maybe Jack will bring you to the party."

"Party?" Jack said.

"Yeah, at Jacinta's—I'm sure you're invited. I'm inviting you! It's on Facebook."

"Okay." Jack rolled back on his heels. "Maybe see you there."

"Very nice to meet you, Miss Ruby," Yacub said, and he wanted to slap himself for that *Miss* but she laughed and smiled and went into the fitting rooms.

Yacub could see that Jack wanted to follow her into the fitting rooms, so he told him he was hungry. Jack paid for the things Yacub had chosen and they made their way to a coffeehouse.

"You'll like this place," Jack said. "Bona fide American."

As Yacub sat on the smooth leather sofa, he contemplated the large pastry and enormous coffee that Jack had bought him. His new clothes—including two cotton shirts with button-down collars, trousers, a zip-up jacket, and a cardigan that Jack had referred to as "preppy"—sat in tidy bags beside his feet in their new socks and shoes. He thought about the girl called Ruby and the invitation to the party, and he found himself wondering if Mrs. Harriet had been correct all along, that he was dead and had entered paradise.

Jack was sitting across from him, tapping away on his phone. When he looked up, Yacub raised his coffee and said, "Thank you, Cousin."

Jack smiled. "Cuz," he said. "Sick."

18

That evening they sat down together for a meal for the first time—Jack, Yacub, Michael, and Harriet. Michael had texted her from work to say his meeting had been canceled. Harriet was pleased; she had cooked roast chicken with potatoes and a dessert and did it herself instead of heading over to the supermarket to buy it ready-made. She set the table with a tablecloth, and then took the tablecloth off—too fussy!—and set the table again. She wanted to find a way to welcome Yacub to the household properly now that he was officially, most definitely, alive. She wore high heels and an apron and felt like Freddie Mercury in that old video. Michael came into the kitchen and looked at her—when he smiled, she smiled too.

Jack and Yacub came in from shopping and went straight onto the games console, so Harriet had to shout at Jack when dinner was ready, just like old times. They sat down and she served the food.

"We'll find you a job," she said to Yacub. He had his mouth full, so he nodded.

"How are you going to find a job for someone who doesn't exist?" asked Jack.

Yacub swallowed. "I exist," he said. "I'm alive."

"I know you exist," Jack said, and to prove it he punched Yacub on the arm, "but not officially."

Yacub looked at him, frowning slightly.

"There are unofficial jobs," Jack said.

"Michael will sort out Yacub's papers. He knows people." Harriet turned to her husband.

Michael raised his eyebrows. "I do?"

"I want to work," Yacub said.

"You can have all the crap jobs that were meant for me," Jack replied. Then he looked at his parents as though he expected them to agree. Harriet laughed, and as she laughed, she felt a surge of love for her son that was so strong she thought she might drown.

19

When Jack got up the next day, Saturday, he noted his father was home. Normally, on the weekend, his dad got up early and threatened to go to the gym, then went to work instead—either in his office upstairs or across London to his actual office. But something had happened in the house without his knowing about it and he needed to stay home to restate his authority or reclaim his territory or something masculine like that, Jack reckoned. By the time Jack got up—he did his best to sleep in, as he knew it was obligatory for teenagers, but he woke up bright and early, always had, always would, and then he lay there, in a kind of daze—both his parents were in the kitchen. Yacub was watching TV. That guy liked to watch TV.

"Game?" Jack asked, getting out the handsets. He hadn't brushed his teeth and his eyes were still crusty but there was nothing better than playing when you were only half awake; the game went straight into your brain, nothing between it and your cerebral cortex.

Yacub nodded and Jack set things up. He could hear his parents talking in the next room.

"Where's the car?" Michael asked.

"In the garage. They said they'd let me know. But it

might be a write-off." Jack's mother paused. "It will probably be a write-off."

"The insurance will cover it."

"Well." Jack heard her pause again. "I didn't report it to the police."

"What?"

"I would have had to tell them about Yacub. And I thought he was dead. I thought—"

"A man falls on your car, and you don't report it?"

"No, I—"

"Jesus, Harriet."

Jack had excellent hearing, even above the sound of the machine gun that Yacub was firing at him. "Hey!" he said, "don't shoot me, shoot the enemy!" Yacub cackled. So Jack shot him and they both went down to zero points and had to start the level again.

"I'll pay for it," Harriet said. "I've still got some of my own money left."

"It's not the money—"

"I didn't know what else to do, Michael. I only did what seemed right."

"Okay," said Jack's father. "All right."

They stopped talking. Maybe they were kissing. Kissing? Jack guessed that was okay. Then the game absorbed him once again. A while later he heard his dad go upstairs to his office.

That afternoon Jack's mother made him cut the grass; she had a long mental list of chores that from time to time she tried to make Jack do. Jack liked the smell of mown grass, though he would never tell his mother that; it made him think of Dukes Meadows. When he came back in, his father and Yacub were sitting at the table talking. Michael was explaining what he did for a living. Yacub looked interested.

"So, basically," Michael was saying, "we assess risk in business finance—mergers, takeovers, buyouts—taking into consideration as many of these factors as possible, reporting to investors, shareholders, the banks, and other financial institutions."

"This is what I would like to do one day," Yacub said. "Actuary." He pronounced the word carefully. "Actuary."

Michael smiled. Jack couldn't think of the last time he'd seen his father look so happy. "It's a great profession," he said, "especially in these uncertain times."

Jack looked at Yacub: you risk your life by stowing away in the landing gear of an airplane, and you want to be an actuary? Jack didn't say a word. He decided it would be a good time to ask his father about tonight.

"So," Jack said, as Michael gave him one of his why-don't-you-want-to-join-my-noble-profession-too? looks. "Yacub and I have been invited to a party tonight."

"Oh yeah?" he said. "Where?"

"I'm not sure yet," Jack said, "I don't have the full details." Since the "events" of two years ago, Jack rarely went out; he could tell his father was pleased by the idea.

"There's a website," Michael said to Yacub, "a good website, with a lot of information about the profession. I'll show it to you."

"Thank you, sir," Yacub said.

Jack noticed that his father, unlike his mother, didn't ask to be called by his first name.

"It should be okay for you to go," Michael said. "Bit of a culture shock, Yacub, but you'll take good care of him, won't you, Jack?"

"You know me, Dad," Jack said. "The perfect host."

20

Emily was Facebook friends with both Harriet and Jack. Jack had accepted a friend request from Crazeeharree a while back before unfriending her, Emily assumed, once he figured out she was his mother, and Emily had friended him at that time. Jack had hundreds of online friends; as far as Emily could see, he was indiscriminate about who he connected with and what information he gave away. So she knew about the party, and she monitored conversations throughout the afternoon to try to figure out if this was one she'd be able to crash. For a while she'd been thinking that a subplot about the son would add to the overall story she was trying to tell in her film. *The son.* She couldn't bring herself to think of him as a possible sibling, that was going too far. Besides, maybe the falling man would be at the party. The falling man. She still could not believe what she had seen. Maybe the falling man would be there, and she could talk to him as well.

Fragments of info appeared on a variety of pages as preparty anticipation built. She had to work to keep up with it all. Jacinta's parents were away but Jacinta changed her mind about hosting the party when she saw word had leaked out. Paula said her dad had offered their house, but everyone knew that meant he'd be there, looming in the hallway like the former police officer he was. Abdul suggested Dukes Meadows, and everyone shouted him down on that, who wants to have a party out there in the cold and the dark, and maybe it would rain? Hetem said why not have it there, no parents, no one watching, no neighbors to complain. A bit more banter and then that was it, decided. Now everyone could invite everyone else without worrying about the party busting down the walls of someone's parents' house.

She looked at herself in her bedroom mirror. Could she pass for sixteen? The sixteen-year-old girls all looked twenty-six, but that wasn't the point. Reverse engineering was much more difficult, especially among teenagers, who have a sixth sense when it comes to "old" people. She couldn't decide if the red hair made her look older or younger. She foraged in her closet for the right clothes. Were girls wearing too much makeup or was it the none-at-all look these days?

She arrived on her bike at dusk and the field was already a sea of bodies. There were three cars parked along the access track at the northern end of the common, behind the trees, their boots open. A crew of older guys was doing a brisk trade selling beer; skinny girls and hefty boys waddled away from the cars, laden with cans. As she watched, they finished up, stocks depleted; they slammed their doors shut and she heard one of them say, "Back later."

She locked her bike, got out her cameras, and went

to work. She took a photograph of the crowd and her flash went off, illuminating the young faces. The people closest to her pointed their phones at the source of light and, Emily guessed, a dozen photos of her appeared on Facebook moments later. She made her way into the crowd.

21

Before they headed out to the party, Jack asked Harriet for money "for food." Harriet always caved at the thought that he might go hungry, and she gave him some cash. He didn't tell her the party was at Dukes; he said it was at Abdul's house, as Abdul had an undeserved reputation for being reliable, steadfast, and sober due to the fact that he came from a reliable, steadfast, and sober Muslim family. She said, "Say hello to Abdul from me," as if Jack would ever do that, ever. "Sure, Mum," he said.

Yacub was dressed in his new clothes, looking very pleased with himself. Harriet lavished him with compliments and he was lavish in return: "Thank you, Mrs. Harriet, thank you. I will pay you back soon," practically lowering his head so she could scratch him behind the ears. Jack was a little worried about what people would say when he turned up with his new best friend; the button-down shirt and brand-new chinos made Yacub look like— well, he looked like an up-and-coming actuary on his day off. Hopefully no one would be that interested in him and, besides, having Yacub with him was definitely contributing to his parents' feeling relaxed and happy about him going out to a party.

Jack had been pretty much grounded since David

McDonald died and he and his mother had their "events." Well, not really grounded, though he used that as an excuse with his friends. He did go out from time to time; he wasn't a complete loser. Truth was, he didn't feel like going out much anyway. He had less freedom than his friends whose parents had eased up after a few weeks of searching, heartfelt conversations about personal responsibility and the whole things-were-different-in-my-day-drugs-were-weaker/nicer/better, etc. But he was used to it now. He'd become sort of housebound, institutionalized; he found it difficult to imagine ever leaving home.

However, seeing Ruby again reminded him of how much fun they used to have together. And then finding out that the party had been moved to Dukes Meadows— well, that was it. Jack had to go.

On their way out they stopped at the corner shop and Jack bought them both a tin of the caffeine drink that the school drugs counselor said contained the equivalent of seven cups of coffee and one cup of sugar. Yacub made a face when he took his first sip, but to his credit he drank it down without spitting it out, which was more than Jack could say for himself the first time he'd tried it. When they arrived at Dukes, it was getting dark, but Jack could see that things had already started. The first person he came across was Frank; he had a huge haul of beer piled up on the ground and he was selling it rapidly.

For months after Jack had passed the bag of weed to Frank and Frank was expelled as a result, Jack had dreaded running into him. He folded it into his overall strategy of staying grounded and not going out much: better that than run into Frank. When he finally did see him—on the high street, with their mothers—he was stunned to discover Frank wasn't angry.

"Hi, Jack," Frank had said.

"Hi," Jack had replied.

"See you around," Frank said, and he smiled.

Jack could not understand why Frank had not told on him. If it had been Jack, he would have squealed like a pig. Jack felt indebted to Frank, though he wasn't about to tell him that. Now, he bought six cans of beer off him and gave three to Yacub.

Yacub looked surprised. Then he said, "I like beer."

Jack wasn't convinced. "I guess they don't drink much in your part of the world," he said.

Yacub shook his head and squared his shoulders. "I like beer."

"Okay then," Jack said. And they headed into the crowd.

It was a mild evening. It hadn't rained much of late, so the ground was hard. They made their way down to the river, which was where Ruby and a few of her friends had been saying they planned to hang out. The crowd was thinner there, so Yacub and Jack sat down and leaned against a tree—at least Jack sat down and leaned against the tree. Yacub didn't want to sit on the ground in his new trousers.

It was great to be back at Dukes Meadows. No one had figured out how to rig up a sound system—bit of an oversight—so though the common was full of people, it was oddly quiet, voices snatched away by the breeze. Some kids were doing that thing of dancing with their headphones on, no one listening to the same music, but they were a bit halfhearted, as though they'd read about flash mobs online but actually doing it was, in fact, really boring. Like so many things in life, Jack thought.

A while later, music started up in the distance; it sounded like it was coming from a car. Jack got up and brushed himself off and suggested to Yacub that they head over. Yacub looked a little reluctant until Jack said, "Maybe we'll find Ruby." Everyone perked up at the thought of Ruby.

22

After the plane had risen thousands of feet into the air and he realized that there was no way off the shelf where he was crouching and into the plane itself, Yacub decided that, if he survived the journey, he would have a beer to see what it was like. Alcohol was illegal in Pakistan, and he hadn't drunk in Dubai, not even when he worked for Imran, who was half drunk most of the time. But on that flight, squashed into a metal corner, he decided he would embrace becoming an American. He would play baseball. And he would drink a beer and raise a farewell toast to the Islamic Republic of Pakistan and no one would arrest him.

And here he was with Jack at a party, his heart already racing. Jack had given him *three* cans of beer and he drank them, one, two, three. He was determined to like it.

Yacub followed Jack through the crowd toward the pulsing bass of the music. On the way they passed girl after girl who looked like Ruby, though none was as lovely. Yacub had seen Western teenagers in movies and on television, though none of them were quite like this. Here people shouted at each other above the noise of the crowd and built pyramids out of empty beer cans before using another can to knock the pyramid over and then laughing like this was the funniest thing they had ever seen. There were couples kissing right in front of everyone else and Yacub even saw one couple lying on the ground together, kissing.

The music was getting louder as they drew closer to its source. But then the sound switched off abruptly, they heard a car door slam and an engine start. As the car pulled away, people shouted and booed, and soon the party was quiet once again but for the noise of talking and, in the distance, girls singing.

There was still no sign of Ruby. A girl with bright-red hair, like hair that had been soaked in blood, came up to Jack; she had a video camera and she was filming him. When she turned her camera on Yacub, he put his hand over the lens. "No thank you," he said. He'd seen Imran do this to a reporter in the hotel.

She persisted in aiming her camera at him. "What's your name?" she asked.

"I will not be giving you that information," Yacub replied.

She lowered her camera. She blinked once, twice. "Are you the falling man?" she asked.

As soon as she said that, Jack stepped between them, and his height completely blocked Yacub's view.

"That's a nice camera," Jack said. "What's your name?" As he spoke he put his hand behind his back and waved Yacub away. Yacub took his chance and slipped into the crowd. He had begun to feel very unwell. He had started to feel very, very unwell indeed.

He went along, trying not to stumble, not wanting to fall onto the ground in his new clothes. There was nowhere to sit, nowhere to go at all, in the darkness and the great heaving mass of people.

Yacub remembered when he flew back from Dubai to Karachi. After he got beyond passport control and through the exit doors, he emerged into a vast crowd, women, children, men, young and old, jammed into the arrival hall, all waiting for some longed-for family member; he'd never seen such a tight-packed crowd of people. The floor was strewn with rose petals and the crowd jostled in the intense heat as they struggled to spot their relatives. He felt happy to be among his own people at the same time as feeling annoyed that there seemed to be no way to get through the crowd, no way at all out of arrivals.

Tonight the crowd was almost as dense, but whereas in Karachi airport everyone was Yacub's color and height and size, here they were enormous, tall *goray* like Jack or tall and black, tall and skinny, but also lots of huge people, people with acres of extra flesh on display, popping out between their T-shirts and their jeans. Yacub was among the giants, all speaking in their indecipherable slang. Having to look up to see their faces was making him feel dizzy.

He stumbled, landing on his hands, which were now covered in mud. When he stood up again, there they were in front of him, the three *desi* boys he had seen in the American shop.

"Oi!" said one. "You! What're you doing here?" Now there were more boys in the group, six or seven, Yacub thought.

"He's got his new clothes on," another said, as though this in itself was ridiculous.

Yacub swayed slightly.

"He's fucking hamstered! A good Muslim, you cunt."

They were also drunk, clutching cans of beer. Yacub found their comments baffling.

"Oi! Speak up," one of them said, but he didn't want to talk to them. The crowd came to his assistance, surging around him, and once again, he disappeared into it. He had to find Jack. In the distance, he saw the trees, black against the night sky. Where was Jack?

23

Harriet was at her workstation in the kitchen, checking her Facebook. The boys had gone out to their party. Michael was slumped in front of the TV, catching up with the shows he had recorded. Jack had unfriended Crazeeharree almost immediately but remained friends with the more recent Tracy Wentworth-Fitch; she half suspected that he knew it was her but chose to ignore that fact.

For the last few years, Harriet had fought against the urge to monitor her son online; she was mostly successful. She wanted him to have his own life, a private existence that she knew nothing about, a rich, complex, and secret realm. The astonishing truth was that he was a good boy.

But this evening, she gave in to her baser instincts. Instead of worrying less because Jack was with Yacub, she found herself worrying more. Someone had witnessed and photographed Yacub's fall. And were they out there, looking for him? She checked her feeds once again but found nothing, so she scuttled around the internet, catching up with the plans for the party. Dukes Meadows. Okay. Deep breath. Jack had said the party was at Abdul's but that didn't matter. At Dukes there was a good chance the police would shut the party down. If that didn't happen, she would get in the car and drive over at around midnight; once there, she'd phone Jack and offer him and Yacub a ride home.

Harriet clicked around the friends' pages. Photos from the party had begun to appear already. Jack wasn't posting photos yet but Harriet saw from earlier postings on his page that he had renewed his acquaintance with Ruby.

Ruby. After that McDonald boy had died at his own party, it transpired that Ruby's older brother was a drug dealer and that he'd been selling weed to Jack, and that they'd been passing around the drugs at school. Frank was expelled, Jack narrowly missing out on expulsion himself, and the name Ruby had become a kind of parental shorthand for "bad news." "Will Ruby be there?" "Is Ruby going?" What these questions really meant was: Will my baby son or tiny sweet daughter be smoking spliff at this party?

But Ruby. Harriet had always loved Ruby, despite all this. How could you not love Ruby? She was gorgeous, and she was very sweet. She made you want to take care of her, with those dark rings under her eyes.

Harriet poked around Ruby's page for a while. She had already uploaded a few photos from the party. None of Jack. Mostly endless shots of groups of girls hugging each other and smiling into the camera, beers aloft. The dark mass of Dukes Meadows behind them, the sky getting a little blacker with each shot. Harriet was keen on the facial recognition software Facebook had implemented a while back; it helped her keep tabs on who was who in Jack's wide circle. A photo appeared of a girl, her bright red hair luminous in the flash, a photo of someone who was photographing the photographer. She looked a bit older, and a bit familiar. Harriet stared at the image. Then the software kicked in and the name appeared on the screen, hovering next to the young woman's face.

It took Harriet a full minute to process this information. Emily. Emily was at the party.

"I'm going to the supermarket," she said to Michael.

"It's ten thirty," Michael said, looking up from the television screen.

"It's open all night on Saturday." Harriet grabbed her bag and went to the drawer where the car keys were kept. "Shit."

"What?"

"I won't be long," she said. "Don't wait up for me." She hoped he'd forgotten about the car. Going out at this time of night without a car would make him think she was having some kind of breakdown. She thought of the moment earlier in the day when she'd kissed him.

Michael let out a dissatisfied sigh as she went through the front door.

The taxi dropped her off on the main road; the lane that runs down one side of Dukes Meadows was blocked with cars, which was not a good sign. It was a mild, bright night for early spring, and although the cars were packed tight, there was no music, which Harriet found disconcerting. As she made her way toward the meadow, a plane passed overhead.

The sound of the crowd rose up on the night air as

Harriet walked down the lane, weaving between the cars. And there it was: in the darkness, a large mass of people stretching all the way to the river, lit only by the screens of their phones, talking and shouting and drinking, at least half of them lost and trying to find each other, phoning, texting, messaging: "Whr r u? Whr r u? Come find me. Find me." The whole of West London youth, gathered together in one place.

She moved forward along the edge of the crowd and thought for a moment that the ground was covered with stardust, but it was beer cans and bottles, thousands of them, carpeting the edges of the field, crumpled and shiny, smashed and glittering, a sound like dull cowbells as they were kicked around. And still no music.

She tried to phone Jack but it went straight to voice mail. She wasn't sure where to go, how to find him, how to find Emily, or even whether she was here to find Emily or to stop Jack from finding Emily—to stop these two lives from colliding.

24

Jack tried to get the girl with the blood-red hair to go away but she wouldn't. He hoped Yacub had understood the international hand signal for "run away." The girl kept filming Jack and asking questions.

"Was that the falling man?"

"He's been known to fall from time to time, if that's what you mean."

"What's your name?"

"What's yours?"

"You're Jack, aren't you?"

"If you know so much already, why are you asking so many questions?" Jack was a bit drunk and thought he'd try being clever, but he was also sober enough to know he wasn't really clever at all.

"You live at home with your mum, Harriet."

She made it sound like Jack was a thirty-year-old who couldn't be bothered to move out because he didn't want to have to do his own laundry. "I'm sixteen!" he said. And now he felt like a total idiot, because this red-haired girl was definitely older, most definitely considerably older, and she'd think a sixteen-year-old was basically some kind of little kid.

"What's Harriet doing these days?"

"Why are you so interested in my mum?"

When Harriet and Jack had their "events," the press had taken an interest. Photographers lurked across the street for a week or so and the tabloids got hold of Jack's phone number and started ringing him. His mum had anticipated this happening, so she'd prepared Jack and he wasn't taken in. Harriet was convinced their phones were hacked as well, so they got new phones and let the old ones sit there on the kitchen counter. They'd ring from time to time and Harriet would shout "Not on your nelly!" and they'd laugh and let the damned things go to voice mail. Jack listened to the messages every once in a while; after a few days the callers started offering money if he'd call them back, but he wasn't tempted. And then, after not too long, the interest in them went away. Harriet was old news. This far down the road Jack thought he would probably have to pay to get a journalist's attention. So why was this girl behaving like she was filming him for some kind of fresh tabloid scoop?

"That's enough," Jack said.

To his surprise, she lowered the camera and smiled. " All right," she said. She held out her hand. "I'm Emily," but she didn't say it in the way most people say their names when they meet somebody. She said it in this over-emphatic special way that meant she expected Jack to slap himself on the forehead and shout, "Oh! *You're* Emily!" as if he'd been waiting his entire life to finally meet her and he was a moron for not recognizing her straightaway. He felt a flash of annoyance and was about to tell her to go fuck herself or, more likely, something much lamer, when he felt an arm slide around his waist.

It was Ruby.

"Bye, Emily," he said, "nice to meet you." He leaned down and gave Ruby a kiss on her lips, and to his astonishment she kissed him back.

"Let's go down to the river," said Ruby.

Jack could tell she had taken something: her eyes were very wide and she was speaking in a breathless way as though her heart was pounding and everything and everyone was tremendously exciting. She was doing this thing that she did back in the day when they used to hang out at Dukes and smoke her brother's draw—she'd fold and thread her fingers together over and over again, as if she was going to say a prayer but decided against it but then changed her mind yet again. And when she walked she held her hands parallel to the ground, moving them from side to side, as though she was about to tap dance or something.

Jack could see that she was heading away from the river—they needed to go toward the big trees, not away from them. The crowd had begun to thin a little, as the thirteen- and fourteen-year-olds finished trashing their young brains before being picked up by daddy at the arranged time and place. In another hour an older crowd would arrive and things would get scary. Jack took Ruby by the hand and turned her in the right direction. They picked up the pace; moments later she stopped short.

"Hey, Jack," she said, reaching into her pocket, "take

this." She unfolded a small piece of foil, licked her finger and stuck a little pill onto one end. She gave him one of her Ruby smiles and said, "Open wide." He hesitated. David McDonald. All the bad things. But then he looked down at Ruby's face. He opened his mouth and stuck out his tongue. Then he closed his lips around her finger. She looked up at him, smiling.

They walked through the crowd and down to the river and all the while he began to feel lighter and lighter. He couldn't stop thinking about Yacub, he couldn't stop imagining what it must have felt like when Yacub was released from the landing gear of the plane and falling. Flying.

When they got down to the riverbank Ruby wanted to sit on a bench and look out over the water. The Thames curved sharply here, and there was a chunk of parkland directly opposite. On the far side—not that far, as the river was fairly narrow at this point—a set of steps led up from the tidal river into the trees. Jack couldn't see the steps, it was too dark, but they were there in his mind's eye. He couldn't see whether the tide was in or out, whether the river was low or high, and he felt the need to know.

"Wait for me here," he said to Ruby, but she didn't answer. She was sitting on the bench and looked like she'd fallen asleep. He scrambled over the railing and down the riverbank, along the uneven ground, slipping on rocks and gravel, through the stinging nettles, brambles, and blackberries. The tide was high, and the river churned past where he stood, and he could hear the water right in front of him, he could smell the wet of it. The party receded. Jack had always loved the Thames, his whole life he loved the river, it was part of why he loved Dukes with its enormous trees and its long grass and its big sky.

So he walked forward, and felt his trainers fill with water. He felt heavier and heavier, more and more weighed down by the water, pulled down into the water, as though by the force of gravity, just like Yacub must have felt as the ground rushed toward him that day.

25

Yacub wandered along the riverside footpath, dodging the revelers, thinking to himself that perhaps the Islamic Republic of Pakistan had got it right and making alcohol illegal was a good idea, though he had stopped feeling sick and now felt—well, he felt happy. He lifted his face to the breeze and smelled the river. The night air was soft and damp in England, and it was as though it washed his face for him, kept him clear and clean, far away from the dust of Dubai, the filth of Karachi. The mud on his hands had dried and he'd succeeded in brushing much of it away. He straightened the collar of his new jacket, adjusted his new trousers. These clothes alone were enough to make him happy. Something inside him had shaken loose, been set free.

He came to a bench to one side of the footpath, over-looking the river, with a girl curled up on one end, her hood drawn over her head as though she was asleep. Yacub felt tired—he was looking forward to the day when he no longer felt tired all the time—as he sat down beside her. The moon had come out and he had a good view of the river. Someone—a man, Yacub thought—was moving through the water, wading in as though he was planning on walking to the other side. The water reached his thighs; he slipped a bit and was suddenly in up to his waist. Yacub sat straighter. It didn't look right. It didn't look right at all. It—it was Jack.

As though she'd heard his thoughts, the girl on the bench woke up with a start and lurched forward.

"Jack!" Ruby screamed. "Jack! What the fuck are you doing?"

26

Harriet didn't think it was possible to feel any older than she felt that night. The teenagers parted for her as though she was unclean. Despite the dark, despite being drunk or stoned or impaired in some way, they could tell she was someone's mum. Harriet made her way across the field. A few times she saw kids she thought she recognized, friends of Jack's, but they moved away from her rapidly, and she knew better than to try to speak to them. She heard an ambulance siren getting louder, drawing near, and she could hear shouting coming from down by the river. She began to run and had to push people out of her way, forcing her body through the crowd, which grew denser the closer she got to the riverbank. She broke through to a clearing and saw the paramedic closing the ambulance doors. A girl was standing behind the ambulance, lit up by red taillights and the blue lights that flashed on the roof of the vehicle. The ambulance gave a short siren burst and began to drive away.

She touched Ruby's arm. The girl looked at her and collapsed in tears. "It's Jack, Mrs. Smith. He got into the river."

"What?"

"I don't know why he went into the water, like he thought he'd go for a swim or something. His cousin went after him and pulled him out—I don't know how—he—"

"His cousin?"

"Yeah, the cousin from Pakistan—"

"Is Jack all right?"

"I don't know, he wasn't speaking. His sister pumped his chest and made him breathe—"

"His sister?"

"With the red hair. She told the paramedic she was his sister. I didn't know Jack had a sister. He was completely drenched and coughing up water and he—"

"Which hospital, Ruby?"

"West Middlesex."

"Go home now, Ruby. Go home."

And Harriet ran up the lane toward the main road, shouting into her phone for a taxi.

27

I open my eyes and then close them again. Too bright.

"Put the camera away," I told her,
"you're not allowed to film in hospitals."

I didn't say her name, not yet.

I open my eyes again. My mum. Who is she talking to?

"Why are you here? You said you're his sister?"

All this time, all this waiting—and
here we are, and she's denying it.
She's denying *me*.

She thinks I'm her mother! Of course—
that was inevitable. How stupid of me.
Crazeeharree.

Crazeeharree. Did she think I'd never figure it out?

Sister? I have a sister? I can't keep my eyes open. It's too
bright.

28

"I understand if you don't want to discuss it in front of him," Emily said, indicating the very long boy on the hospital bed. They were separated from the rest of Accident and Emergency by curtains.

"I followed you online," Harriet said. "I'm not proud of it. But I needed to see you, to see how you were doing. I've worried about you all these years."

"You followed me online and you're still going to deny it?" Emily said.

"Deny what?" said Harriet. "You're not his sister."

Harriet watched Emily crumple. Her clothes were wet; her mascara had leaked down her face. She put the camera on the plastic chair by the curtain, pulled a soggy tissue out of her pocket, wiped her nose, and began to cry.

"You look like her," Harriet said. "You look just like her."

Emily looked up. "Like who?"

"Like your mother."

29

Jack surfaced once again and fought to open his eyes. His mother and that girl with the red hair were still standing beside his bed. They had their arms around each other. They were hugging. Shit, they're crying. Just when it looked as though everything was going to be all right. Fuck, he thought. I must be dead. I've gone and died.

PART THREE

NUCLEAR FAMILIES

AUTUMN 2014

1

Before Yacub arrived, Emily made sure the room was spotless. She cleaned the window for the first time in a long time, sitting on the sill and leaning back carefully to spray and wipe the glass outside as well. She removed evidence of her own life, so as not to distract him. Sofa, empty side table. Camera on the tripod, clip-on micro-phone ready. The big lamp on its stand. Earlier, she had gone to the supermarket to pick up tea, milk, and bis-cuits to offer him, to make him feel welcome. As she paid for her purchases, she listened to the many tills beeping, and remembered the day Yacub landed in the car park. A lot had happened since then. And now she had a whole week off work to film the interviews. Emily couldn't bring herself to add up the number of years it had taken for her to reach this point; her friends had long since given up asking about *Me, Myself and I*. But she was nearly there now. Nearly.

What was this film about, exactly? Family. Sort of. Belonging. Not belonging. Harriet. Her film was about Harriet, really. And the falling man.

She'd rehearsed them a bit, over dinner at their house, tried to give them a few tips on how to talk to the camera. Not Harriet, of course, she was a pro, but everyone else.

She'd told them to talk freely, to open their mouths and let the words fall out. "I'll edit," she said, "I'll cut and crop and make sure you look and sound your best." They'd looked at her, en masse, from around the table—Harriet, Michael, Jack, and Yacub—their faces grave. "Oh come on!" she said. "It'll be fun!" She could see they did not believe her.

But now everything was ready. She stood by the window. Winter was closing in and the trees across the swath of southwest London were mostly bare. Yacub was coming on his own today; she'd have to wait till he arrived before she could finalize the lighting. She moved around the room, adjusting and readjusting.

The doorbell rang. She buzzed to let him in.

He was dressed neatly, everything ironed, his button-down shirt looking brand-new. He kept swallowing hard as though his throat was dry, and he couldn't seem to look her in the eye. These days, most people were keen to be filmed—people filmed each other all the time—and she'd forgotten that not everyone felt comfortable sitting in front of a camera.

She filmed him standing beside the window. She pointed out the supermarket and asked him to look in that direction. He obliged. Her efforts to help him relax with tea and biscuits and chatter did not work. So she sat him down. He was sweating under the strong light, so she offered him a bit of powder and makeup, and he submitted to her ministrations. He looked good on camera. She framed him through the viewfinder, his brown skin and black hair, his white shirt contrasting well against the burnt red of the sofa, the dark green of the wall, the whole thing warm and serious. They were ready.

"I'm going to turn on the camera and keep filming while we talk. You can say whatever you like, you can tell me whatever you want. Don't worry if you make a mistake—just start over again. I'll edit the film and cut out any mistakes. All right?"

He nodded.

"Let's test the sound levels."

"What?"

"Say something to me so I can check the sound."

He looked around the room. He looked at the floor. "That's a nice carpet," he said.

"It's a flying carpet," she said. "I'll lend it to you if you like."

Yacub laughed.

"Okay," she said. "Let's start at the beginning. How do you like living in England?"

He took a deep breath, looked at the camera, and began to speak. "England is kind of a . . . a funny country, but I'm getting used to it. It's not as funny as Pakistan, mind you." He smiled.

Emily smiled back, encouraging him.

"Actually, to tell the truth, I steer clear of 'England' and stay in London. Michael took me to Leicester with him once, on business, a day trip. Have you been to Leicester?"

"I'm going to try to keep myself out of this," Emily replied.

"What?" said Yacub.

"I'm not in the film. It's just you talking. Anything I say will be edited out."

"Oh."

Yacub looked pained, so Emily decided she'd better reply to his question, try to get him to relax. "I've been to Leicester, for work," she said, "but I've never spent any time there. On the last series of *Ginger* we had two Asian girls from Leicester, so I went up to talk to them before we started filming. But I don't know the city."

"Why do you take people who dye their hair red as well? Their hair was hennaed."

"I know," said Emily, "it doesn't seem right. But otherwise it is very . . . well, culturally limiting."

"Too many Scottish people."

"Yes," Emily said.

Yacub was satisfied.

"Start your sentence again."

He looked puzzled.

"You were saying you went to Leicester with Michael?" Emily prompted.

He adjusted his posture and began to speak once again. "I went to Leicester on a day trip and was shocked by all the *desi* midlanders, their clothes gray and black, none of the colors of their homelands—or their parents' homelands, grandparents' homelands, great-great-great-grandparents' homelands either." He stopped, as though momentarily awed. "Anyway, I decided against going to study in Leicester and stayed in London, which as far as I'm concerned is a good thing. London is the place to be."

Emily held her breath, willing Yacub to keep talking.

"The Smiths took me in. They have been so kind to me. It's as though because they were at war with each other—" Yacub stopped himself and looked annoyed at what he'd said. "Despite Jack almost drowning, and the whole business with you—"

Emily interrupted Yacub. "Don't mention me."

"Why not?"

"Just try not to mention me. If you do need to mention me, refer to me as Emily."

"Oh," said Yacub. "Okay."

"Okay. You were talking about the Smiths and how kind they were despite the fact that they had troubles of their own."

"Did I say troubles? I don't think I said that." Yacub adjusted his posture, doing up the top button of his shirt, then undoing it again. "It was as though they had to focus their kindness somewhere, and so they focused it on me. While they were busy being"—he paused to choose his words—"cross with each other, they were nice to me."

He opened his mouth to continue to speak, and then stopped. He rearranged himself on the sofa, sitting up straight, lining up the creases in his trousers.

"My mother used to tell me tales of djinn and fairies. I loved her stories. Although I'm young, I've already had many lives—my father's village, Karachi, Dubai, and now London, England. And that's just me. If we add in my sister, and Mrs. Harriet, and Michael and Jack and"— he paused again and blinked slowly—"Emily—already that is too many stories. There is no room for all these stories.

"I'm studying now, which is what I've always wanted to do. However, because my education was so"—he turned toward the window—"brief, I have a long way to go before I will arrive at that splendid day and qualify. In the meantime, I am catching up, taking exams, working on my English. Michael knew a lawyer and they helped me sort out my papers. I have a job now. I send money home to Raheela—that's my sister. I pay my rent to the Smiths. I'm a good worker. I work at a coffee counter in Heathrow, Terminal Five. In fact, I'm a manager there now." A look of amazement flitted across his face. "A manager."

"That's great, Yacub, really great. Thank you."

"We're stopping?"

"No, no, I just want to change the direction of the conversation a little." Emily looked at Yacub through the camera's viewfinder. The lighting was still fine. "Let's start from the beginning."

"The beginning?" Yacub asked. "I—I'm not sure— I—" He cleared his throat. "The first person I met when I arrived in London was Mrs. Harriet."

"Pakistan," said Emily. "Your life in Pakistan before you arrived in England."

"Mrs. Harriet and Jack's father have been exceedingly kind to me. They could not have been any kinder."

Emily calmed herself. Let him talk, she thought. Let him say whatever he wants, whatever he needs. Edit later.

"I did not want to come to England. I thought I was

traveling to the USA. I wanted to go to America for a new life."

"What's wrong with life in Pakistan?" Emily asked.

Yacub gave her a look of disbelief.

"I love my country," he said. "It is dear to me. The mountain valley where I grew up is very beautiful. Our lives were hard, but our lives were good as well, at least they were before, when I was a child. I would have been happy to have stayed there, to have taken care of my sister, to have married."

"But instead you are here. Why?"

Again, that same look.

"Tell me what it is like where you come from. I've never been to Pakistan. Where did you grow up?"

"My family grew red onions in the Swat Valley."

"Red onions?" Emily said in a tone she hoped was encouraging.

"When you think about Pakistan, all you think about is disaster and terrorism, the American raid on Bin Laden, who we were either too stupid or too corrupt to catch ourselves, blasphemy trials and forced marriages, floods and earthquakes, religious murders, our politicians gunned down by their own bodyguards." Yacub stopped.

"That's right," said Emily. "We don't know any better."

"Or the so-called Pakistanis that you have here in Britain, with their mashed-up slang and their curries and their gold chains and their low-slung jeans."

Emily looked out from behind the camera and nodded.

"When I think of Pakistan, I think of red onions, the piles of red onions getting bigger and bigger as we worked on the harvest, the smell of them, the stains from their skins and flesh on my hands. And the tall trees in the wide valley where my family labored, the mountains towering over us, keeping us safe, and my father, and my mother, and my sister."

He looked at the window again. "I sent her a new phone. Raheela. We talk online. Our uncle is working on getting her married. I'll go home for the wedding."

He looked up as though there was something to see other than the gray London sky. "The seasons progressed in a regular rhythm in our village, and in the spring you've never seen a sharper contrast between the green of the fields and the blue of the sky. Our village was so small that when I was a child, there was only one phone, but no one could afford to use it, so mostly it sat there, forgotten. We didn't need phones. My sister used to run down the road ahead of me—she was always faster than me, even after I grew taller than her . . ." He stood up abruptly, the unit for the wireless mic falling out of his pocket, pulling the mic off his lapel. He walked rapidly across the room to the window.

Emily could see he was doing his best not to cry. She wondered if the mic would still pick up what he was saying.

"I do get homesick," he said, "even though I'm happy here."

Emily nodded.

"I miss my sister."

"I miss my father," said Emily. "He's been dead for four and a half years but I still think of him every day. You would have liked him. He'd have liked you."

Yacub, pulling himself together, turned toward her. "My father would have said you were a harlot infidel beyond all imagining."

"*Inshallah*," Emily replied.

2

Emily and Jack got on well, mainly because of the effort that Emily had made to put him at ease. She never presumed with Jack—she never presumed with any of them—but it wasn't long before she could see that Jack did presume with her, and this made her happy. He presumed that she'd have time to see him, he presumed she was interested in his life, he presumed that their relationship didn't require a lot of effort and energy and thought. He was eighteen, ten years younger than Emily. He had finished school and was working for a year before heading off to university, but he maintained a lucky child's assumption that he was loved. He considered Emily to be part of his family, and this made Emily happy as well, regardless of the tensions and stresses in her dealings with other members of the family, regardless of the fact that they were not related. With Jack, things were easy.

She set up the room carefully, as carefully as she did for Yacub, though this time she left things much as they were normally, stuff piled on the side table—bound books, a couple of print magazines, her tablet—and her laptop on the floor. It was a small flat, and she was not fond of clutter; most of her stuff was digitized anyway. She'd bought two packets of those sticky Belgian waffle biscuits she knew he liked, and a big carton of smoothie, and a couple of beers for later.

He was at the door. She put on her lipstick before she let him in.

He was reluctant to take his coat off, keeping his hood up over his head, and he wouldn't sit down. "What do you want me to talk about? Is this about the adoption thing?"

"No, not at all." She hadn't expected him to be defensive. "I want to hear what you think."

"About what?"

"Your family."

"My family? Oh jesus. That's boring."

"I don't think so."

"You've never lived with us."

Sometimes when she was over for supper and she watched them—Harriet, Michael, Jack, Yacub—and how they got along, despite or because of everything, she did wonder what it would be like to live there. She could occupy one of the many rooms; she could leave her shoes by the front door. She wouldn't be alone. No, she liked being alone. Well, most of the time.

Now Jack looked ashamed at what he'd said. Emily couldn't help but smile at him. The thing about Jack was that he was sweet, he was sweet-natured and kind, and she saw that now he was worried he had offended her or upset her in some way by pointing out the obvious. She got up and went into the kitchen, leaving him to stew for a few moments. She returned with the biscuits and the smoothie. When food was on offer, Jack was a pushover—mainly because he was always hungry. He'd do anything for some biscuits and a smoothie.

"Have a snack while I sort out the lighting," she said.

He nodded and adjusted the tray she'd presented him with. "You want one?"

"You go ahead."

While she was fiddling with the lights, Jack relaxed a little. She placed her chair behind the camera and without telling him started to record.

He cracked his knuckles, one at a time.

He stretched out his long legs and rolled his head to ease the tension in his neck. Not for the first time Emily thought, It can't be easy being so tall. Nothing in the world quite fits. Clothes. Chairs. Doorways. Other people.

"Ruby and I broke up," he said. "You're not filming yet, are you?"

"No."

"I don't know why we even tried going out—hopeless."

"Why did you do it, then?"

He gave her a look. "It's Ruby. She'll always be—I don't know—it's like she is Essence of Girl to me. She'll always be. Despite everything."

"I'm sad to hear it didn't work out. I like Ruby."

"Everyone likes Ruby. But the girl has— Well, she has troubles."

"How long had you been seeing her?"

"We weren't really seeing each other. We went out on a date. That was it. But I had high hopes. Ridiculously fucking high hopes. As always. Why do I have such high hopes all the time? What is it with me?"

"You are one of life's optimists, Jack. You always have been, you always will be."

He shook his head. "So uncool."

"Okay," she said, pretending to put the camera on. "Tell me about that night at the river. Tell me what happened."

"That was a long time ago."

"Two years," she said, "not so long, really."

Jack lowered his head. She was worried for a moment that he wasn't going to talk. But then he brought his head back up and looked toward the window. The light was perfect. "Yacub flew. The man's a genie. Or he's a cat with nine lives, most of which he's already used." He stopped.

Emily leaned forward. "Start at the beginning. That evening. That party."

"Where I met you for the first time," he said.

"That's right."

"Well, it's all been documented already. It's in the police report."

"I want to hear it from you."

"The party on Dukes Meadows. I took Yacub with me. He'd only recently . . . disembarked, as he says. I'd run into Ruby the day before—I hadn't seen her for ages—and she invited us to the party."

"Yes."

Jack drew a breath and then spoke quickly. "Yacub and I drank a few beers, we met you, you were overly interested in Yacub, you knew he was the falling man, and that was alarming. I didn't know who you were, so I hadn't even had a chance to be alarmed by that as well." He stopped and looked stricken. "What if I'd tried to hit on you or something gross like that? Oh my god, it doesn't even bear thinking about."

Emily laughed. "I wouldn't have let you. I knew who you were. At least, I thought I knew who you were."

"Oh yeah," he said. "Okay."

"Let's leave me out of this for the time being."

"What do you mean?"

"I don't want you to talk about us—you and me. I want you to focus on the river. And Yacub."

"Oh," he said, "okay." He looked across the room. "Yacub and I drank a few beers, then Yacub wandered off, and I ran into Ruby. Ruby gave me— Well. This has been documented already, like I said. Ruby gave me a tablet, she wasn't sure what it was, some kind of amphetamine. Some kind of hallucinogenic. A pill—a fucking powerful pill. I took it. I don't know why I took it—I should have known. I'd avoided taking things like that before . . ."

He looked at Emily. She wondered what he wasn't saying.

"A bit of draw, a few beers, the odd swig of vodka. I'd never taken anything, you know, chemical." Jack's face reddened, and he covered his mouth with his hand.

"What is it?" Emily asked.

"We don't really learn from other people's mistakes, do we? Otherwise there'd be no more wars and shit." He cleared his throat and gave himself a little shake. "You'd think I'd be big enough—physically large enough—to absorb such a thing without losing my mind. But no. I'm six-five, with the constitution of a fairy princess. Ruby and I went down to the river; I think all Ruby wanted to do—she'd taken it as well, remember—was sit on a bench and watch the night pass by. But I, well, I decided I needed to get into the river. The River Thames . . . I'd never been in the Thames."

Jack had forgotten about the camera. He addressed Emily directly. "Have you been in the Thames?"

"Yeah, I have. There's a place near Henley that I've been to a couple of times with friends."

"Really?"

"Yes—I'll take you there sometime."

"That would be good," Jack said. "I'd like to have another go at it. Maybe without having on five layers of clothes and my trainers."

"It's a promise," she said. "Start again."

"Oh, yeah, okay."

"'I'd never been in the Thames,'" she prompted.

"I'd never been in the Thames. Getting into the water felt like the best thing I'd ever done. I had this idea that the river would be shallow and warm, with a smooth, sandy bottom, and that those steps on the other side were easily within reach." He slumped slightly on the sofa. "I don't know where I got that from—shallow, warm, with a sandy bottom. When I was a kid—nine or ten, I guess—my parents and I had a holiday in a fairly remote part of Spain, sort of the middle, near the border with Portugal, and we found all these beautiful wide, empty, sandy-bottomed rivers. Nearly every day we'd go for a swim and have a picnic. My dad was really happy on that holiday. He said that his love of swimming in fresh water, in rivers, in lakes, was the thing that made him feel most Canadian. My mum and I laughed at him. But I knew what he meant. There's something about clean, fresh water that makes you feel alive.

"But the Thames is none of these things—it's tidal, it's muddy, it's rocky, it's full of debris. People have been chucking junk in that river for thousands of years. And it's deep, and there are powerful currents. It's much wider than it looks, even at that narrowish point by Dukes Meadows. It's also freezing. It was spring—it was a warm night, but the water was cold. The weird thing was that I didn't notice any of this. To me, the water was warm and placid and soothing. It felt fantastic. The sound of it alone—that volume of water." He stopped.

Emily waited.

"The water. The suck and hum of it." He paused again. "I was in the water for a long time. It felt like a long time. Standing there—struggling to stand—but standing, nonetheless. The sky above me. The breeze. Little waves slapping against me.

"Then I heard shouting. Ruby's voice. Shouting my name. So I turned to see where she was—I had this lovely image in my head of Ruby in her swimsuit, coming to join me—and that's when I lost my footing and fell in. Right under. Mouth full of water. Trying to get a foothold. Struggling. Slipping. I remember thinking, I've got to swim, jesus it's so fucking cold, I've got to swim to the riverbank. But my clothes—those giant trainers, my fucking hoodie . . .

"Shit," he said. "I'm sorry. Are you going to have to bleep all that swearing?"

"Don't worry, I'll deal with that. My target audience is not children."

"Your target audience," Jack said. He became serious. "You think people will want to watch this?"

"That's my aim," Emily said. "But we're a long way from that. Don't worry about the swearing."

"Okay." Jack took a drink of smoothie.

Emily watched while he composed himself.

"I kind of woke up then," he said. "At least, I realized where I was and what was happening. I thought I was going to drown. I kept being pulled underwater by the current, slipping and sliding, trying to find a foothold in the mud and the stones and the crap; just when I'd think I had my footing, the river would shift and I'd go under again and when I came up I'd be farther away from the shore. I could see that people were running along the embankment, shouting. I was lucky the moon was out that night. And then I saw him."

Jack stared at the wall blankly. He looked down at his hands.

Seconds passed, a minute. Two minutes. Jack shuddered, cleared his throat, ran one hand up and down his face, rubbed his eyes.

"He kind of flew toward me—Yacub. I don't know how else to explain it. He was on the riverbank one moment, down at the edge of the water. I saw him before I went under once again. I was really losing it now. I'd swallowed a ton of water and my clothes were fucking heavy, and all of a sudden I was so tired, I— Well. I went under and when I came up he was swooping across the water toward me, and then he had me under the arms and—jesus, I'm nearly twice his size—and he hauled me out of the water. The moon was out, but it was dark and windy and— The next thing I knew I was in the ambulance and the crew was fussing over me and I was throwing up, and you were there.

"You were there, and when they tried to make you leave, you said you were my sister. That's what you said. And I was puking and coughing and freezing and still thinking I was about to die, but through all that I looked at you and I thought, I remember thinking, My sister, and here I am about to die. And then I thought, jesus fuck, Mrs. Harriet is going to kill me."

Jack smiled, and then he grew serious again.

"He's a genie, that's what I tell him. He doesn't like it when I say that. But there's something, isn't there, something. Some kind of magical power. How else can you explain it? He survived that journey in the underbelly of the airplane. He fell out of the sky and onto my mother's car. And before that, if you talk to him about his background, he survived so many things. Get him to talk about it. Magic. At least that's what I think. No one agrees with me. Least of all him. Not even Ruby, and she was there that night.

"It doesn't say anywhere that he flew into the river. It's not in the police report." He looked at the window, into the sky. "But I saw him."

3

Emily got along well with Michael, but mainly because she flattered him by asking him for financial advice and, subsequently, acting on that advice. When her father died, she inherited a savings bond that matured soon after; she'd been sitting on the money. Michael had helped her invest it. He told her that he was impressed that someone so young was interested in her financial future. She wasn't interested in her financial future; she was interested in getting along with Michael, so it had been a good investment. She thought that when Michael thought of her, if he thought of her at all, it was with a certain degree of fondness.

Of all her interviewees this week, it had been Michael who was the most difficult to persuade. "No," he'd said the first time she asked. "No, not me."

"But I need you to talk to me. If you're not there, a piece of the story is missing."

"This is about you and Harriet," he said. "It's not about me."

"But you are important to the story. Look," Emily said, "you might as well agree now. Otherwise, you'll have to put up with my badgering until you do agree."

"Why?" Michael asked. "What can I add? What is this documentary about, anyway?"

She badgered, and eventually he agreed.

She opened the door to him. He came straight in, took off his jacket and sat on the sofa. "Is this where you want me?" he asked, rolling up the sleeves of his white shirt. He was on his way home from work.

She looked at him through the camera. "Shift a little to your right, please."

He shifted. She could smell the day on him.

They spoke at the same time. "So . . ." Emily began.

"Let's get started," Michael said.

"Okay," she said, and she pressed record.

She looked at him through the viewfinder. "Wait a minute." She adjusted the lighting. Michael sat very still on the sofa, legs crossed elegantly, one arm along the sofa's back. She looked at him again through the view-finder. The effect was odd. She was startled by what she saw—Michael was one of those people, surprisingly rare, who look better on camera than in real life. The combination of lens and lighting did something to his face, made his skin look luminous, made the bones beneath his skin appear sharper, his whole face more focused. He'd got back into shape since they'd first met; he didn't look any younger but had become handsomer somehow. He looked relaxed and at ease with himself in a way she would never have anticipated.

"Okay," she said again.

Michael looked at his watch.

Emily felt slightly panicked. "You've been very kind to Yacub."

Michael gave her a yes-of-course-what-did-you-expect look.

"Not everyone would have been so kind."

"I wasn't exactly thrilled when I first discovered Harriet had brought him into our home. But once he was there, not even I was heartless enough to throw him out onto the street. And Harriet, well, don't forget, she'd been unemployed for two years then."

Emily thought about Harriet.

Michael continued. "She needed a project. No, that's wrong. Damn." He shifted in his seat, looking pained.

"What?" said Emily.

"Sometimes when I talk about my wife I sound so patronizing. The truth is, *I* needed a project. We both did. Helping Yacub sort himself out— God, now that sounds *really* patronizing."

"Start again," said Emily. "Start again."

"Harriet had not had a great couple of years. Being unemployed did not suit her. It wouldn't suit me either— neither of us, we're not hobby people. We don't have *interests*. We like our jobs. We like our home. We like our son. We watch a bit of TV. We read. We go to the odd movie. Harriet inhabits the internet. I read the financial pages." He laughed, then stopped abruptly. "We're not itching to get on with that thing we've been putting off all our lives, like some people—I don't know—write that novel. Genealogy. Gardening. That kind of thing. If I got fired, I'd be one of those men who dresses for work every morning for the job that no longer exists and then sits on a park bench while trying to figure out the most efficient way to kill myself."

Michael took a deep breath, uncrossed and crossed his legs. "You're young, Emily, and you've never been married," he said. He looked rueful.

She didn't reply. Unlike the others, Michael didn't seem to need her to reply. For all his reluctance, he was a natural.

"Marriage is, well, it's kind of epic. It *is* epic. You forget about it for years and years, you carry on living together, when your kid is small, while you're both working, the sports days, the school plays, the anniversaries. The fucking anniversaries. That's when it hits you. That's when you think—hoo boy. Year after year. The person you're married to has become like part of your own body, except separate, and at times annoying. There. There all the time. No question about that. The truth is it can be a bit dull. If you let it."

He rubbed his hands up and down his face. "Why am I talking about marriage? I look at you and I feel the need to talk about my marriage. Sorry. Edit that bit out. Please."

"Don't worry about it."

"Marriage is not easy. How can something that's so much a part of the fabric of your life be so difficult? God."

He looked away, toward the window. "Jack's going to hate this."

"What do you mean?"

"We had a tricky time, Harriet and I, a few years back. My fault, of course, but not entirely. There was always something else, something that came between us. Jack was getting older and turning away from us."

"Can you be more specific?"

Michael smiled at the camera. "No," he said.

And the interview was over as quickly as it had started.

4

Harriet arrived, apologizing for the two large shopping bags full of food. "It's one of the good things about being back at work," she said, "no time to go to the supermarket."

Emily laughed.

Harriet handed her the bouquet of flowers she'd bought for her and gave her a kiss on the cheek. "Lovely to see you," she said.

Emily breathed in Harriet's perfume. "Thanks for coming."

"I don't have long," she said. "I have to get home and cook supper for the boys."

"Can't the boys cook for themselves?"

"They can," Harriet said with a nod, "but there's no food in the house."

"Can't they do the shopping?"

Harriet gave her a look.

Emily ducked her head.

"Come on," Harriet said, "let's do this thing."

Emily took the flowers into the kitchen and put them in the sink. Harriet carried the shopping into the sitting room and placed the bags on the floor, on either side of where she sat on the sofa, like protective buttressing or sandbags.

"You can leave those by the door," Emily said.

Harriet shook her head. "They're fine here." She looked down at the bags. "Sorry," she said. "That's weird." She got up and moved the bags near the front door before sitting down once again. "Michael told me it wasn't too bad," she said, "your interview. He said he waxed philosophical on the topic of marriage." Harriet winced. "Was it okay?"

"He was great. He's coming back for more on the weekend."

"Okay," she said. "I'm nervous."

"Would you like a glass of wine?"

"A glass of wine!" Harriet said. "Good idea."

Emily returned to the kitchen, took the cork out of the bottle, and poured two large glasses of white wine. Her hands shook.

In the sitting room, Harriet drank a mouthful and closed her eyes and breathed deeply. "Kate Winslet," she said. "Gather. Gather."

"What?"

"Oh you know, Oscar speech. The camera, brings out the diva in me. Maybe I'll explode in a frenzy of swearing. Cause another YouTube sensation."

"Don't worry," said Emily. "There won't be any of that."

"Any of what?" said Harriet.

"Clips on YouTube. At least not from me."

"Outtakes? Bloopers?"

Emily shook her head.

"Turns out I'm much happier behind the scenes."

"Me too," said Emily.

"Okay. What do you want me to talk about?"

Emily drew a breath and took another sip of wine. "Let's talk about my mother," she said.

"This is our subject, isn't it? Yours and mine."

Emily nodded.

"This time for the camera," Harriet said.

Emily nodded again.

"You do realize that I think of you as a kind of daughter?"

"And I thought of you as my mother for a couple of years before we met. Hard to shake."

"I know," said Harriet. "I'm sorry. That whole following me, friending you business."

They fell silent. Emily shifted forward to turn on the camera. "Whenever you're ready."

"I'm ready." Harriet cleared her throat and pushed her hair away from her face. "The short version. Okay?"

"Okay."

"We were housemates. Your mother and me. She was the best friend I'd ever had. I loved her the way only a twenty-year-old can love somebody—I gave it everything I had. No one else mattered to me. Then she met George Sigo. He was a lunatic." She put her hand over her mouth. "I can't say that. You'll cut that, won't you?"

"Yes," said Emily.

Harriet started again, speaking rapidly. "She ditched him, finally. But she was pregnant. Then she had the accident. She fell. You were born, but she died. I took you home with me and took care of you for a whole week. Her parents decided to put you up for adoption. I tried my best to keep you, I tried to get my parents to help me, but no one listened. I had no rights. And then you were gone. It was too late."

Harriet picked up her glass and knocked back the rest of the wine. "More, please," she said.

In the kitchen, Emily cut herself on a sharp bit of foil on the wine bottle. She ran cold water over her finger, dripping blood on the big yellow daisies in the bouquet she'd left in the sink. She thought about how in the first interview she'd tried to stop Yacub from including her in what he was saying. So much for that. She'd heard Harriet's story before, many times. But that didn't stop it from feeling like having her bones scraped with a razor blade.

She wrapped her finger in paper towel, filled Harriet's glass, and took it to her. Harriet was gazing toward the window. The camera was still running.

"That was a bit brutal," Harriet said. "I'm sorry."

Emily sat down. "When you're ready."

"We were twenty years old. We were students at what was then the Polytechnic of Central London. Journalism. Both of us. Me and your mother, Elizabeth Barry. Barry. She called herself Barry, so we all followed suit, though she was the least Barry-like person around. I guess she thought Barry would make her seem less posh. She wasn't posh—her background was like mine, ordinary suburban London girls. We came from opposite ends of the Northern Line, Morden in her case, High Barnet in mine—but she was one of those Englishwomen who seem posh no matter what they do.

"We were all, I don't know, what's the right word? Adventurous. The Poly was a hotbed of radical politics, and it was the nineteen eighties, after all, plenty to be angry about. We were angry. But we also had this incredible freedom. I'd spent my first year commuting between college and home every day but then I met a bunch of people who were squatting in Vauxhall, near the river, and they invited me to move in. They'd occupied a series of big houses in a terrace. An enterprising New Zealander called Mick—they were all enterprising, those Kiwis, they knew how to make stuff, unlike us Brits, we were useless—anyway, Mick had carved out an amazing room in the attic of one of the houses, all built-in shelves and a raised platform to sleep on, beneath a skylight that gave onto a little wild roof garden he'd planted.

"Mick got beaten up on an estate in Stockwell when he was trying to rescue a broken chair from a skip and he'd decided to go back to New Zealand. His room was vacant. I jumped at the chance, though I had to lie to my parents about it being a shared rental—they would have been horrified by the idea of me squatting. I had a bank account with the post office—god, I'm so old, it's like I'm talking about the Dark Ages; you had to go in and stand in a long queue with your payment book—and I used to deposit the rent check they sent me every month. I used that money to pay for—"

Harriet's grip tightened on the edge of the sofa.

Emily said, "Do you want a break?"

"I spent that money on flowers after she died, Emily. Six enormous bouquets of the most extravagant flowers in the whole of South London. Elton John for a day. She would have laughed. I don't know where I thought they would go because her parents dealt with her funeral—in the end I filled her room full of flowers. I used to take you in there to feed you." Harriet smiled. "There was a famous actress called Elizabeth Barry. Restoration. Did you know that? Barry used to mention it but then she began to think it was part of what made people think she was posh, so she stopped."

Emily said, "I looked her up online."

"Did you?"

"Not the best-looking woman."

Harriet laughed. "Barry used to claim she was descended from her. No idea if it was true. But Barry, well, the main reason people thought she was posh was because she was so beautiful. Those classic English rose looks. You have that, Emily. The fine white skin. The symmetrical features—the straight nose, the clear blue eyes, that hair that's somehow always silky and smooth. You look so much like her."

"It's a Brazilian blow-dry."

"Pardon?"

"It's this hair treatment I get every six months or so," Emily said. "It's a chemical blow-dry that makes your hair smooth and silky. Takes hours and costs a fortune."

"Oh," said Harriet. "Well, that's disappointing."

"Is it?"

"I thought you were a natural beauty."

"But I am," said Emily.

"What else is fake? Come on, tell me."

"Nothing!"

They both laughed and paused and drank.

"You really were my baby, for a while at least, for a whole week."

Emily looked at Harriet. She wished she could remember it. With all her heart she wished she could remember being three days old and being held by Harriet. She felt tired. "Okay," she said, "that's enough for today."

"Okay," said Harriet. "Do you want to come home with me for dinner?"

"Not tonight."

Harriet began to take off her microphone.

"Hey," said Emily. "One more question? It's not one we've discussed."

Harriet sat back. She looked nervous. "Yes?"

"Your own parents. Why are you so . . . detached from them?"

Harriet let all the breath in her lungs go in one long sigh.

"I'm sorry," said Emily. "Big question. You don't have to answer."

"It's okay. The answer's simple, really. You were denied your family, so why should I get to have one? I was angry. I was twenty. They were hard on me."

Emily did not reply.

"I have to go cook for the boys."

5

"I don't have much to say. What's there to say?" Jack looked straight at the camera. "What do you want me to say?"

"Tell me what life at home is like now that you've finished school and are working."

"Okay. I can do that."

Jack seemed more relaxed this time. He'd made a bit of effort with his clothes, had done away with the hoodie. "Ready when you are," Emily said.

"For a couple of hours I thought you were my sister."

"It was nice, wasn't it?" Emily asked.

"It was. A sister! But I also thought I was dead. Neither turned out to be true. But since then you sort of have become my sister. And Yacub, he's a kind of brother. I still tell people he's my cousin. They look at me, they look at him. It's entertaining.

"It's good at home. It's so much better than it was two years ago. Mrs. Harriet's working again, which is a huge relief for us all—she's no longer quite so *Crazee*. Dad trundles along as he always trundles along but he's home more, not at work all the time, and he makes an effort with Mum—it's kind of sickening, but it's also sweet. He gives her flowers. They kind of date, in a weird way. They go out to the movies or into town to see an exhibition on the weekend. For a while I thought my family was going to break apart. But that hasn't happened. Instead it's been transformed, it's grown—first Yacub, then you. We've expanded. You should get married and have some kids, Emily, and you should all move in with us."

There it was again, that moving-in idea.

"It's a good idea," Jack continued. "You're not getting any younger."

"Thanks, but I don't think Michael would want me and my growing young family moving in with you."

"You never know. He can be quite sentimental at times. Also, it's a Pakistani tradition, isn't it, the big extended family, and we're honorary Pakistanis now, according to Yacub. Mrs. Harriet would love it. And anyway, I'll be gone soon."

"Off to uni."

"Off to the debt factory."

"You'll come back, though. I can see it already. You're definitely going to be a stay-at-home adult child."

"You're probably right. I'll move my growing young family in as well. I'll have such a massive debt from my ten years at university that I'll never be able to afford to leave."

"Well, it's a plan," said Emily.

"Not really," said Jack. "Not really."

6

On Saturday, Emily got up early and went for a cycle along the river. She felt apprehensive; today she was interviewing Harriet and Michael together. This had been Harriet's idea, and Michael was happy to oblige. Emily figured it might prove fruitful.

It was windy along the river and rain spat at her intermittently, but she kept up a good pace and was soon sweating inside her cagoule. The sky was gray and the river was gray too, the colors of London. The trees were stripped of their last remaining leaves, and the wind pelted her with them. She decided to get away from the embankment and onto a road. She found herself cycling across the river, toward Chiswick New Cemetery. She'd visit her dad, and she'd tell him everything.

She'd showered and finished her breakfast when her doorbell rang. She opened the door to Michael and Harriet. They looked smaller somehow, thinner and more tentative than usual. "Hello!" she said, sounding falsely hearty. "Come in! Welcome!"

They entered the flat, bumping into each other, bumping into the walls of the narrow corridor. Harriet had brought a cake for Emily. "I actually made it," she said, "I didn't buy it."

"It's true," said Michael.

"I'll make coffee," said Emily. "We'll have cake."

Harriet looked satisfied. They walked into the sitting room, where the camera and the big light on its long-legged tripod were already set up.

Michael stood by the window. "You have a great view from here," he said. "Haven't been here during daylight."

"You can see the supermarket," said Harriet.

"Oh yeah," said Michael, "look at that."

"I filmed Yacub falling from here," said Emily. She put her laptop on the table and pulled up the file. She played the footage. Yacub falling. Yacub landing.

"My god," said Michael.

"You've seen it before, haven't you?" Emily asked.

"No," said Michael. "No, I haven't."

Emily glanced at Harriet, who shook her head. "It's not something—" Harriet said. "You sent me a copy but— I mean—I don't think Yacub's seen it either."

The footage continued. Harriet standing there, her trolley escaping. Yacub getting up. The mini-cab arriving.

"Jesus," said Michael. "Fuck."

"It will be in my film," said Emily.

"I suppose so," Michael said. "Can't see how you'd resist that. Of course, if anyone asks, we'll say it's faked. For the purposes of added drama or something."

"It's easier to believe it's fake," said Harriet. "If that wasn't me standing there, I would think it was fake."

"That *is* you standing there, isn't it?" Michael asked.

"Yes, it is," said Harriet. "It's me."

"What happened to that car?" asked Emily.

"It was totaled. A write-off."

Michael gave a small, disapproving huff.

"I'll make coffee," said Emily.

They sat down on the sofa.

When Emily returned from the kitchen, Michael had his arm around his wife's shoulders, their bodies connecting neatly, both equally ill at ease.

"Okay!" said Emily.

"Listen," said Harriet, "I'm just going to start talking, okay? If you want me to stop, interrupt or something. But I'm going to try to say it all, go through once while you film without stopping. Okay?"

"Sounds good to me," said Emily.

"Michael will stop me if I say anything stupid. Won't you?"

"That's what I'm here for."

"All right," said Harriet.

"Okay," said Emily. She turned on the camera and gave Harriet a nod.

"I kept you secret all those years. It wasn't really a secret, I just didn't tell anyone about you. Nor your mother. And somehow because I didn't tell anyone for so long, it became a secret. My secret. The thing I had never told Michael. I don't know why—I was ashamed. I was ashamed that I hadn't managed to convince them to let me keep you, though looking back, there was no chance of that happening, and it seems strange that I convinced myself it was a possibility. I was ashamed that you'd been given up to people none of us knew. And I felt guilty for not preventing it from happening—the accident, I mean. I felt guilty for not preventing Barry from getting involved with George Sigo. And afterward, George was in prison, and I didn't want to have anything to do with him, and then when I did— Well, that was a bad idea."

Harriet took Michael's hand; he was looking toward the window. He looked at the camera, and then at his wife. Emily thought, how handsome he looks in this picture.

"So I kept it secret. I tried to contact you through social services at one stage—I knew your birth name. Barry had always said if you were a girl you'd be called Emily. I made an appointment and they got out your file, and I managed to see your real name—your new surname—written across the top before the woman realized I had no right to the information. After that I was stuck for a long time. I couldn't figure out how to contact you. If you went looking for your birth mother, the trail would not lead to me. George's name wasn't on the birth certificate, so the trail wouldn't lead to him either. I kept it secret, it was too peculiar, and what would Michael have thought about my having kept it secret all those years? So, eventually, I began stalking you online.

"Okay," said Harriet. "Okay."

"Another coffee?" Emily offered.

"No," said Harriet. "I'm fine."

"Michael?" said Emily.

He was staring out the window. He looked back at Emily. "Yes?"

"Can you tell me what you thought about Harriet's secret?"

He looked at his wife.

"You were accepting at the time," said Harriet. "We'd had a bad couple of years before that, you got stuck in Toronto and—"

"I got stuck in Toronto and when I got back, things were difficult between us."

Harriet looked at her shoes.

"Come on," said Michael, turning back to Emily and the camera. "This is excruciating. I don't want to talk about that. I didn't like the idea that Harriet had carried the weight of this secret all that time. I was glad she told me."

Harriet took his hand and squeezed it and began to speak again. "I told you about the room I had, Mick's amazing room, up in the attic. Well, Barry had the same room, in the house next door. Hers was not nearly as nice—they'd laid a plywood floor, but the roof beams and struts were bare. Freezing in winter, boiling in summer. And no window, just one or two bits of Perspex shoved in place of the roof tiles. I guess whoever had lived there before had been good friends with Mick, because they'd knocked a small opening into the brick wall that separated the two houses, beside the chimney breast, and put a miniature door there, a little cupboard that you'd open expecting to find a fuse box or something, but instead you'd find a view into the room next door. And that's how I met your mother. The day I moved in, I opened the little door and Barry was standing there on the other side, looking through. I screamed and slammed the door shut. When I opened it again, she was still standing there, smiling. For a moment I wondered if the little cupboard housed a portrait, like Dorian Gray before it all went wrong, a portrait of a beautiful young woman. But then she spoke.

"'Hello!' she said, and she stuck her hand through the gap. 'I'm Barry. You're my new neighbor.' We arranged to go to the pub together at lunchtime—" Harriet looked at Michael. "God, remember going to the pub at lunchtime?"

Michael shook his head. "I never went to the pub at lunchtime."

Harriet looked back at Emily. "And that was that. I fell in love with her and we became best friends. Barry had other best friends, she had a lot of friends, she collected people, and she liked nothing so much as to introduce them to each other. But Barry was it for me. We glued ourselves together, cycling up to the Poly for classes, heading over to the South Bank to go to old movies at the National Film Theatre, pottering along the mucky strand by Vauxhall Bridge when the river was at low tide, spending hours in the pub with our friends. At night we'd leave the little cupboard door open, and we'd lie in bed and talk to each other through the open space.

"On the river near where we lived there was an enormous abandoned building, a giant storage facility—Nine

Elms Cold Store, it said, in big letters across the top. It was an enormous box sitting there by the river, with these thin slatted windows or airbreaks of some kind. It had a central core that was empty, cavernous—it hadn't been used as a cold store in years, and no one knew who owned it. It was dark and cold and the concrete floors were full of vast unanticipated holes and puddles. It's long gone, demolished to make way for flats. We used to have parties there. It was a renegade space—we were squatters. We liked to pretend that anything that wasn't occupied was ours for the taking.

"It was at one of those parties that Barry met George Sigo. With his black Irish good looks. He was London Irish, a Catholic, a Republican, but he was clearly unwell in some fundamental way—subject to rages. Obsessions and rages. You could feel it in him once he'd had a few drinks. He'd get into fights. I never could see what Barry saw in him—all I ever saw was that rage. He was involved with Troops Out." Harriet stopped. "Do I need to explain what Troops Out was?"

Emily shook her head.

"He used to spend half his time cooking these horrible meals to deliver to the Republican prisoners who were on remand in Brixton Prison." Harriet looked at Michael as though she expected him to say something. He pursed his lips.

"Anyway, George cooked his meals, and Barry helped him when she had time—she even helped him deliver them to prison occasionally. She was devoted to him. At least, she was devoted to him for a few months. And then she stopped being devoted to him. And George stopped coming round. It was very abrupt. She wouldn't tell me what had gone wrong—she looked pained when I asked her and said it was in the past, it was over, it had been a mistake, George was a mistake and she didn't want to think about it any longer. I accepted that. Why wouldn't I?

"And then after another few weeks she realized she was pregnant. *Quite* pregnant. Had been pregnant for some time. But even that didn't seem to faze her. Her plan was to continue with her course: she'd have her degree by the time you were six months old, she'd do the work placements that were part of our course, and she'd find a job, easy. I admired her for that. If I'd got pregnant then, I wouldn't have even considered keeping it." Harriet gasped and covered her mouth. "Shit, I'm sorry."

Emily shook her head. "Don't worry, I'm not offended."

"Listen," said Michael, "have you got any beer?"

Both women looked at him.

"It's nearly lunchtime," he said. "All that talk of pubs."

"I've got some in my fridge."

"Please," said Michael.

"Harriet?"

"Oh, not me."

Emily went into her kitchen and opened the fridge. She had made contact with George Sigo about a year after she met Harriet. It went okay. He was out of prison again but he was struggling. She hadn't enjoyed feeling sorry for him, and he'd gone out of his way to make it clear they owed each other nothing. "I just wanted to lay eyes on you, girl," he said. "I've done that now."

She'd allowed Harriet to take her out to dinner after the meeting. They'd ended up in the ladies' room, Emily crying so hard they both thought she'd be sick. When she could speak, she said, "I really am an orphan, aren't I?"

Harriet gave her another hug. "Nearly," she said. "Not quite."

Harriet appeared at her side now in the kitchen. "Do you have any more of that wine we were drinking the other evening?"

When they returned to the sitting room with their glasses of wine, Michael stood up to stretch and drink his beer.

Harriet sat down. "I went on a bit there. Sorry."

"I thought it was good," said Emily. "Interesting."

"You're probably the only person in the world who finds this interesting."

"Could be."

"I'll continue." Harriet looked at Michael.

"Be my guest," he replied, and he sat back down beside her.

"Barry was healthy throughout the whole pregnancy. She bloomed, she really did, like only a young pregnant woman can. She had pots of energy too—for college, for our social lives, for having fun. For me. The little door that had been shut while George Sigo was around was open once again. Six months, seven months, eight months—she got bigger, but she was slight, like you, she never really seemed that large, that pregnant.

"It was close to Christmas, and before everyone set off to see family, we decided to have one last big party at the cold store. Somebody was friends with somebody else who was in a band—a big brass punk band, if you can imagine such a thing—and they set up their stage down one end of the vast room. At the other end, which was partially open to the river—I guess there'd been a dock there at one time, but most of that was gone, only a few pilings still standing—we made a big bonfire. And hundreds of people came. The band played, and we danced, and we stood around the fire trying to get warm, and we drank cheap cider and punch made from the cheapest red wine. Barry wasn't drinking, at least not more than a glass, and that was part of what made the accident so inexplicable.

"At the back of the big room, high up above the stage, there was a series of platforms—I guess what was left of the cold storage units. There was a rickety set of stairs. It was late, really late, around three in the morning, and I had got very cold—it was so cold inside that building, whatever time of year—and I was thinking about heading home. The band, or at least part of the band, was still playing. I looked up and I could see that a large group of people had climbed up to the platforms and they were dancing. I saw Barry, she was up there dancing alone, doing a kind of slow gyrate with her hands on her belly. I called up to her and waved, but the music was too loud, she couldn't hear me.

"And then it happened. The little platform she was standing on gave way, right beneath where she was dancing. She fell through the air. I saw it happen. I looked up and she was falling. She looked surprised, not frightened, just sort of—hey, what's this? She was falling. Falling. She hit the side of the stage and landed half on it, half on the floor. The band stopped playing."

Michael took her hand.

Emily stared into the viewfinder, afraid to look up.

"She fell through the air. She landed hard," Harriet said, her voice soft. "She did not get up and walk away."

Emily knew the story, Harriet had told it to her a few times, but never like this, so plainly.

"Somebody ran out into the night to find a phone to call an ambulance. Someone else tried to move her, but she screamed and we all shouted at him to stop. I rushed to her and stroked her hair and held her hand and talked to her. She was conscious, but not really. A lot of blood from where she had hit her head. But the worst thing was the way she was lying, half on, half off the stage, like a broken thing, a broken doll.

"The ambulance came, and I went with it. You were born. And Barry died."

Through the camera, Emily could see Harriet's eyes glinting, heavy.

"Turn off the camera, Emily, please."

Emily turned off the camera, and Harriet turned to Michael. He drew her close, and she cried. Emily could hear her, and she could see her shoulders heaving. She got up to fetch a box of tissues from her bedroom. Before returning to the sitting room, she opened her drawer and pulled out the old yellowed Polaroid that Harriet had given her not long after they met for the first time. In it, Barry was laughing. She was wearing a flowery summer dress with spaghetti straps and a wide-brimmed straw hat. The sun was shining and beyond the flowers was a view of London rooftops. On the back was an inscription in Harriet's handwriting, "Vauxhall, spring 1986: Barry, in our wild rooftop garden."

7

Yacub was Emily's final interview, the last interview she was going to do for this project. One more interview, she told herself, then that was it.

He came in and sat down on the sofa straightaway. Though it was Sunday morning, he had to be out at Heathrow for work that afternoon. "Turn the camera on, I'm ready," he said.

Emily obeyed. "You know, it turns out you're my nearly brother, in a way," she said, "according to Harriet and Jack."

"Nearly brother," he said. "Almost cousin. My *gora* family."

"My colleague, Rob—"

"Who is this Rob?" Yacub asked. "You keep mentioning him. I hope you aren't considering some kind of involvement with this man prior to introducing him to us?"

"I'll bring him next time I come for tea."

Yacub nodded, satisfied.

"Rob went to Pakistan to film for the BBC recently."

"Oh?"

"He had an amazing time; he wants to meet you. Anyway, he said the two things he noticed most while he was there—"

"Apart from the extreme danger and violence and desperate poverty?"

"Apart from that—was the fact that the whole time he felt like a giant white alien, and that Pakistanis are world-class experts at staring."

Yacub laughed. "It's a funny thing, isn't it. It was something I learned when I was working for Imran in Dubai. Not everyone in the world is as happy to stare or be stared at. This is something at which Pakistanis excel."

"Rob rather liked it. He said he figured that if everyone felt free to stare at him with such dedication, he was free to stare right back."

"Stare right back!" Yacub repeated. "Good idea."

"Okay," said Emily, indicating the camera.

"There isn't really anything more to talk about, is there?" Yacub asked.

"Isn't there?"

Yacub spread his hands and raised his eyebrows.

"I have a theory," Emily said.

"I'm not a djinni," Yacub replied. "I'm not dead either."

"I might have never met Harriet if it wasn't for you."

Yacub shook his head. "You'd been following each other for so long, at some point you were bound to collide."

"Maybe. I saw you fall. And I know you saved Jack's life. And Harriet and Michael—you helped them."

"No. They are married. They are happy."

"What do you really think about all of us, Yacub?"

He shrugged. "I'm here. This is where I belong."

"Do you think?"

Yacub shrugged again. "Sometimes. Some days."

"Tell me about when you were on the plane, Yacub."

A frown passed across Yacub's face. "What plane?"

"Tell me what it was like on that tiny metal shelf above the landing gear beneath the belly of that airplane."

8

Emily sat staring at her computer screen. Three hundred and sixteen hours of footage, including all the covert filming she'd done between 2010 and 2012. Another hundred and twelve hours of filming since then. Two thousand five hundred and fifty-seven photographs. Twelve hours of Emily's own straight-to-camera narration. Seven interviews. It was all there. The story of Harriet, Michael, Yacub, and Jack. Her story, Emily's own story, the story of her birth mother, and Harriet, and . . .

It was impossible. She hadn't begun to edit and already she felt defeated.

Work on *Ginger* was, as always, very busy, and now that Emily had been promoted, she often worked a six-day week. Time off was exceedingly precious. Once the current series began to air, with its new, more elaborate punishments, more than half of the participants had tried to pull out, and it had become her job to keep them sweet, to prevent them from leaving. One girl, whose name was Edna and whose long, wavy hair was like spun sugar flavored with mandarin, completely otherworldly, had dyed her hair black. She showed up on the set a few days after walking out, wanting to return, and the executive producer threatened to sack her. Emily persuaded him to keep the girl on—her hair would grow out, which was almost a storyline in itself, and she still had those mandarin eyebrows, those eyelashes, those freckles. Why anyone would agree to be on the show was beyond Emily, but she was good at her job.

She thought of her father. "Get on with it, girl," he'd say. She thought of the silver-scaled coffin he was buried in. It did make her laugh now; enough time had lapsed. He'd be pleased.

Okay, get on with it. She opened a new document. I'll do it. I'll do it the way I know best. The reality show version. Do a draft script and a rough edit. Then at least I'll have something to work on, something to work against. Something to show for myself.

OUR STUFF AND OUR THINGS

SPRING 2015

TITLE SCREEN:

                         FALLING
               a documentary by Emily Barry

A CLOSED LAPTOP. Anonymous hand opens screen.
Browser opens to YouTube. Video begins to play
in browser:

A TOWN HALL full of ballot boxes, party supporters, election officials. Beside the stage, a
MIDDLE-AGED WOMAN in a dark red jacket.

                   MIDDLE-AGED WOMAN
          Here at Tipton Mallet—a town unaccustomed to
          media attention—the battle for votes has
          been intense. Last year's unfortunate death
          of the Labour incumbent, Simon Taylor, MP for
          25 years, combined with the accusations of
          Conservative Party HQ interference in candi-
          date selection, and the unexpectedly high
          ratings in the polls . . .

VIDEO GOES FULL-SCREEN and plays out until
MIDDLE-AGED WOMAN is tackled by MAN (2 minutes)

BLACK SCREEN

VIDEO CLIP of MIDDLE-AGED WOMAN leaving her
house, getting into her car and driving away.
(45 seconds) (SPRING)

VIDEO CLIP of MIDDLE-AGED WOMAN leaving her
house, getting into her car and driving away.
(30 seconds) (SUMMER)

VIDEO CLIP of MIDDLE-AGED WOMAN leaving her
house, getting into her car and driving away.
(15 seconds) (WINTER)

VIDEO CLIP of MIDDLE-AGED WOMAN leaving house,
getting into car and driving away. (SPRING
AGAIN) CAMERA follows behind, weaving in and out
of traffic, falling back, catching up at stop
signs and traffic lights. Follows car into
SUPERMARKET CAR PARK. MIDDLE-AGED WOMAN parks
car, gets out, and walks into SUPERMARKET.

CUT TO: Footage filmed from block of flats.
MIDDLE-AGED WOMAN exits SUPERMARKET with a
trolley full of shopping.

CUT TO: FALLING MAN footage—FALLING MAN dropping through sky.

BLACK SCREEN

REPLAY: FALLING MAN footage played out once again—this time all the way until he lands on car.

CUT TO: FALLING MAN standing beside window, looking out. CAMERA follows his gaze out the window. PAN of London suburb, ZOOM into SUPERMARKET CAR PARK.

CUT TO: FALLING MAN sitting on the sofa.

> FALLING MAN
>
> England is kind of a . . . funny country, but I'm getting used to it. It's not as funny as Pakistan, mind you.

CUT TO: JACK on the sofa.

> JACK
>
> He kind of flew toward me—Yacub. I don't know how else to explain it. He was on the riverbank one moment, down at the edge of the water. I saw him before I went under once again. I was really losing it

now. I'd swallowed a ton of water and my
clothes were fucking heavy, and all of a
sudden I was so tired, I— Well. I went
under and when I came up he was swooping
across the water toward me, and then he had
me under the arms and—jesus, I'm nearly
twice his size—and he hauled me out of the
water.

CUT TO: HARRIET on the sofa, MICHAEL watching
her speak.

> HARRIET
> She fell through the air. I saw it happen.
> I looked up and she was falling. She looked
> surprised, not frightened, just sort of—
> hey, what's this? She was falling. Falling.

BLACK SCREEN

A PHOTOGRAPH—YOUNG WOMAN, smiling, wearing a
summer dress with spaghetti straps and a wide-
brimmed straw hat.

CAMERA REMAINS on still PHOTOGRAPH

> MIDDLE-AGED WOMAN (VOICEOVER)
> There she is. Your mother. You look just
> like her.

ACKNOWLEDGMENTS

The story of Yacub and his fall to earth was inspired by an article by Esther Addley and Rory McCarthy in the *Guardian*, published in 2001. The digital fiction project I developed with Chris Joseph, *Flight Paths: A Networked Novel*, grew directly out of discussion around this story; more than one hundred people participated in the first iteration of *Flight Paths* and I am indebted to them all, including the project's funders, Arts Council England, and supporters: De Montfort University's Institute of Creative Technologies, Refugee Week, and New York's Institute for the Future of the Book. Documentation of this iteration of the project, as well as *Flight Paths* itself, can be found at www.flightpaths.net

Invaluable advice on the novel as well as its digital companions has come from many places and people, including Chris Joseph, Andy Campbell, Martha Kearney, Mandy Rose, Mahvesh Murad, Sara Schilt, Sue Thomas, and Tom Mellor. Kat Meyer and Peter Brantley's invitations to TOC NYC and Books in Browsers in San Francisco have furthered my knowledge of writing, books, and the digital immeasurably; Sophie Rochester and Joanna Ellis of the Literary Platform, and our project, the Writing Platform, have been a constant source of inspiration. The Electronic Literature Organization's inclusion of *Flight Paths* in the *Electronic Literature Collection*, Volume Two, has been vital.

ACKNOWLEDGMENTS

The British Council sent me to Pakistan in 2011; I learned a huge amount from my wonderful hosts and the students I met in Karachi and Lahore. First readers for the novel included Lesley Bryce and Aamer Hussein; their enthusiasm regarding the novel and its structure was crucial. I'd like to thank my agents, Rachel Calder and Anne McDermid, as well as my editor, Nita Pronovost, for their excellent feedback and support. But my biggest thank-you is to my family, Simon, Tom, and Iris Mellor.

ABOUT THE AUTHOR

KATE PULLINGER writes for both print and digital platforms. In 2009 her novel *The Mistress of Nothing* won the Governor General's Literary Award for Fiction. Her prize-winning digital fiction projects *Inanimate Alice* and *Flight Paths: A Networked Novel* have reached audiences around the world.

As well as *The Mistress of Nothing*, Pullinger's books include *A Little Stranger, Weird Sister, The Last Time I Saw Jane, Where Does Kissing End?*, and *When the Monster Dies*, as well as the short story collections *My Life as a Girl in a Men's Prison* and *Tiny Lies*. She cowrote the novel of the film *The Piano* with director Jane Campion.

Kate Pullinger was born in Cranbrook, British Columbia, and is currently a Professor of Creative Writing and Digital Media at Bath Spa University. She is married and has two children. Find her at www.katepullinger.com.